# 1859

*Dear Diary,*

*I've wrapped myself up in a blanket of grief, not letting anyone close to me, not even my dear husband, Daniel. He has grieved, as well, silently, stoically, in the way of men. Daniel has been so patient with me, but I know he feels my distance.*

*Still, as the sun settled on the horizon this morning, shedding its light and awakening the world, life flickered anew inside me. Love for my husband and the possibility of happiness filled the empty spaces that had kept me in the darkness, in isolation, for so long.*

*Daniel, my heart, my husband. We have survived so much, the long and strange journey to this vast, new land; yet, I know our love is strong.*

*Now I must go. I am eager to once more be the woman Daniel needs, the woman he loves, the woman he married before all that we have been through. I am eager to start my new life with my husband....*

Dear Reader,

Oh, baby! This June, Silhouette Romance has the perfect poolside reads for you, from babies to royalty, from sexy millionaires to rugged cowboys!

In Carol Grace's *Pregnant by the Boss!* (#1666), champagne and mistletoe lead to a night of passion between Claudia Madison and her handsome boss—but will it end in a lifetime of love? And don't miss the final installment in Marie Ferrarella's crossline miniseries, THE MOM SQUAD, with *Beauty and the Baby* (#1668), about widowed mother-to-be Lori O'Neill and the forbidden feelings she can't deny for her late husband's caring brother!

In Raye Morgan's *Betrothed to the Prince* (#1667), the second in the exciting CATCHING THE CROWN miniseries, a princess goes undercover when an abandoned baby is left in the care of a playboy prince. And some things are truly meant to be, as Carla Cassidy shows us in her incredibly tender SOULMATES series title, *A Gift from the Past* (#1669), about a couple given a surprising second chance at forever.

What happens when a rugged cowboy wins fifty million dollars? According to Debrah Morris, in *Tutoring Tucker* (#1670), he hires a sexy oil heiress to refine his rough-and-tumble ways, and they both get a lesson in love. Then two charity dating-game contestants get the shock of their lives when they discover *Oops...We're Married?* (#1671), by brand-new Silhouette Romance author Susan Lute.

See you next month for more fun-in-the-sun romances!

Happy reading!

*Mary-Theresa Hussey*

Mary-Theresa Hussey
Senior Editor

Please address questions and book requests to:
Silhouette Reader Service
U.S.: 3010 Walden Ave., P.O. Box 1325, Buffalo, NY 14269
Canadian: P.O. Box 609, Fort Erie, Ont. L2A 5X3

# A Gift from
# the Past

## CARLA CASSIDY

SILHOUETTE *Romance*®

Published by Silhouette Books

**America's Publisher of Contemporary Romance**

SILHOUETTE BOOKS

ISBN 0-373-19669-5

A GIFT FROM THE PAST

Copyright © 2003 by Carla Bracale

This edition published by arrangement with Harlequin Books S.A.

Visit Silhouette at www.eHarlequin.com

**Printed in U.S.A.**

**Books by Carla Cassidy**

Silhouette Romance

*Patchwork Family* #818
*Whatever Alex Wants...* #856
*Fire and Spice* #884
*Homespun Hearts* #905
*Golden Girl* #924
*Something New* #942
*Pixie Dust* #958
*The Littlest Matchmaker* #978
*The Marriage Scheme* #996
*Anything for Danny* #1048
*\*Deputy Daddy* #1141
*\*Mom in the Making* #1147
*\*An Impromptu Proposal* #1152
*\*Daddy on the Run* #1158
*Pregnant with His Child...* #1259
*Will You Give My Mommy a Baby?* #1315
*‡Wife for a Week* #1400
*The Princess's White Knight* #1415
*Waiting for the Wedding* #1426
*Just One Kiss* #1496
*Lost in His Arms* #1514
*An Officer and a Princess* #1522
*More Than Meets the Eye* #1602
*††What If I'm Pregnant...?* #1644
*††If the Stick Turns Pink...* #1645
*A Gift from the Past* #1669

Silhouette Shadows

*Swamp Secrets* #4
*Heart of the Beast* #11
*Silent Screams* #25
*Mystery Child* #61

*The Baker Brood
‡Mustang, Montana
††The Pregnancy Test
†Sisters
**The Delaney Heirs

Silhouette Intimate Moments

*One of the Good Guys* #531
*Try To Remember* #560
*Fugitive Father* #604
*Behind Closed Doors* #778
*†Reluctant Wife* #850
*†Reluctant Dad* #856
*‡Her Counterfeit Husband* #885
*‡Code Name: Cowboy* #902
*‡Rodeo Dad* #934
*In a Heartbeat* #1005
*‡Imminent Danger* #1018
*Strangers When We Married* #1046
***Man on a Mission* #1077
*Born of Passion* #1094
***Once Forbidden...* #1115
***To Wed and Protect* #1126
***Out of Exile* #1149
*Secrets of a Pregnant Princess* #1166

Silhouette Desire

*A Fleeting Moment* #784
*Under the Boardwalk* #882

Silhouette Books

*Shadows* 1993
"Devil and the Deep Blue Sea"

The Loop

*Getting It Right: Jessica*

Silhouette Yours Truly

*Pop Goes the Question*

The Coltons

*Pregnant in Prosperino*

Lone Star Country Club

*Promised to a Sheik*

---

## *CARLA CASSIDY*

is an award-winning author who has written over fifty books for Silhouette. In 1995, she won Best Silhouette Romance from *Romantic Times* for *Anything for Danny*. In 1998, she also won a Career Achievement Award for Best Innovative Series from *Romantic Times*.

Carla believes the only thing better than curling up with a good book to read is sitting down at the computer with a good story to write. She's looking forward to writing many more books and bringing hours of pleasure to readers.

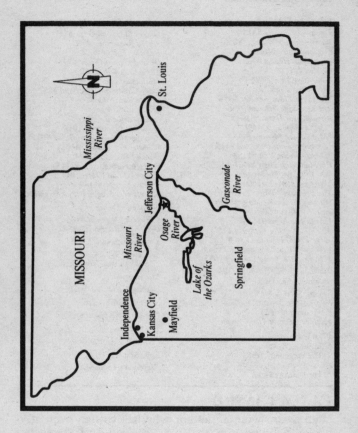

# *Chapter One*

Claire McCane looked like a bag lady. But, as far as she was concerned, most amateur treasure hunters looked like street people. Of course, the small town of Mayfield, Missouri, didn't draw many true treasure hunters.

It had only been since Clark Windsloe, owner of Windsloe Automotive and the mayor of Mayfield, had begun the Pot of Gold contest that the citizens of Mayfield had transformed themselves from ordinary people into half-crazed puzzle-solvers and earth-diggers.

The final three clues leading to where the ten-thousand-dollar treasure was buried would appear in the Saturday morning paper over the next three weeks, but Claire thought she knew where to find the windfall. And heaven knew she could use a windfall.

She briskly walked across the large expanse of manicured lawn that surrounded the two-story brick building that housed City Hall and the police station. She didn't want to draw attention to herself, didn't want anyone else to know where she was going to hunt for the buried money.

Behind the city building were thick woods and it was there she was headed, to the base of a certain tree. Unfortunately she hadn't been able to afford one of those treasure-finding machines with all their bells and whistles. She was armed only with a trusty spade and a healthy dose of excitement.

The late June air felt hot on her shoulders and was sweetly fragrant with the scent of the blooming flowers surrounding the building. As she left the well-trimmed grass for the taller, more tangled underbrush of the woods, she glanced at her wristwatch.

Time was of the essence. She always felt guilty leaving her grandfather in anyone else's care for any length of time. Thank goodness for Wilma Iverson, her neighbor who was available to sit with Sarge.

It was cooler here, with the canopy of leaves overhead to shade the ground. The tree she sought was on the far side of the wooded area, a tree scarred by lightning that had been referred to as the Dragon Tree when she was a child.

The clue in the paper that morning had been something about the roots of fire and ash yielding sweet fruit. She had instantly thought of the Dragon Tree. She desperately hoped she was right. She had a hundred plans for the money if she managed to find it.

She quickened her pace, ducking beneath tree limbs, picking her way through vines and brush, hoping she was the only one who had thought of the lightning-scarred tree.

She heard him before she saw him, somewhere ahead of her, like a bear lumbering through the brush, only there were no bears in Mayfield. At the same time, she became aware of the faint scent of expensive cologne lingering in the air.

Somebody was after her treasure. She quickened her pace, dismay sweeping through her. If she could get to the tree first and get her spade in the ground before whoever was in the woods with her, the treasure would rightfully be hers.

The tree was just ahead when she heard the sound of a shovel hitting the ground. She halted, disappointment crashing through her, then continued forward, intrigued to see who had beaten her to the punch.

As she stepped closer to the tree, she spied him. His back was to her and he was far too well-dressed for a treasure seeker. Dark-blue dress slacks encased long muscular legs and slim hips. A white dress shirt stretched across an impossibly broad back, the center of the shirt damp with sweat.

"Looks like you beat me to the punch," she said dispiritedly.

He whirled around to face her, and she gasped and stumbled back a step as shock riveted through her.

"Joshua." She whispered his name as she stared at the man she hadn't seen for five years, the man who had been her husband...the man who was *still* her husband.

"Hello, Claire."

His voice, that deep, whisky voice, raked millions of unwanted memories through her at the same time as his eyes, as green as the woods that surrounded them, swept over her from top to toe.

Defensive walls shot up inside her. "What are you doing here?" she demanded, irritated by the fact that just for a moment she'd wished she was wearing something other than her oldest pair of jean shorts and a T-shirt streaked with the remnants of white paint.

He gestured to the shovel stuck in the ground. "I'm treasure-hunting."

He certainly didn't look as though he needed to find a treasure. The loafers on his feet looked Italian and had probably cost enough to keep her and Sarge in groceries for a year.

Somewhere in the back of her mind she realized she was in shock. The last person she'd expected ever to see again in her life was Joshua McCane. "I meant, what are you doing here...in Mayfield. Nobody told me you were in town."

He pulled the shovel out of the ground and leaned it against the base of the tree. "I got in late last night. I had coffee this morning in the diner and read the clues to the Pot of Gold contest and thought I'd try my luck in figuring it out."

"Why don't you go try your luck someplace else? This is where I was going to dig." She sounded like a petulant child and she wasn't sure what she resented most, the fact that he looked like a million dollars or that he was thwarting her chance to gain ten thousand dollars.

"It appears I beat you to it, Cookie." To accentuate his point, he grabbed the shovel and dug into the earth at the base of the tree.

She bristled at his use of her old nickname, the one he used to call her when his eyes were lit with love or fired with passion—the name he'd used when he'd loved her...when she'd loved him.

"What are you doing here?" she demanded once again. She didn't want him in Mayfield, and she certainly didn't want him here at the Dragon Tree.

"I told you, digging for treasure." He scooped up a shovelful of dirt and threw it to the side, the muscles of his tanned forearms taut with the exertion.

"I mean, what are you doing back in Mayfield?'' He was being thick on purpose, not answering the question she was asking.

His gaze met hers, a stranger's eyes holding her captive. ''I decided it was time I came home.''

She leaned against the tree trunk. Her legs felt shaky and she wasn't sure if it was from shock or anger. Time he came home. He had no home here, at least not with her. She watched him dig for a moment. ''I can't imagine Mayfield would hold much appeal for a jet-setter like you.''

''Ah, you've been keeping tabs on me.'' He flashed her a quick grin.

The passing of years hadn't diminished the force of his beautiful smile, and she felt it stab her deep in the pit of her stomach. ''Not really,'' she returned unevenly, although it was a lie. ''You know Mayfield. People like to gossip and you've become something of a folk hero…the bad boy who made good.''

Sun drifting through the leaves played on his dark hair, and she saw that he needed a haircut. For most of their life together, Joshua had needed a haircut. Her fingers tingled for a moment with the memory of his thick, rich strands of hair beneath her fingertips.

Resentment ripped through her and she pushed herself off the tree trunk. ''You don't need this money, Joshua. Why don't you go away and let me dig?''

He glanced at her once again, but continued

shoveling. "You wouldn't need this money if you'd cashed the checks I've sent you over the years."

"I didn't want your money." She hadn't wanted anything from him after he'd left her, and all she wanted from him at the moment was for him to go away.

"How's Sarge?"

"He's fine. We're all fine, and now you can go back to California or London or wherever you came from." Again she heard the petulance in her voice and she hated herself for it, hated him for creating it.

"Is he still keeping the streets of Mayfield safe from crime?" he asked, obviously ignoring her outburst.

It took her a moment to realize he was talking about Sarge. Apparently he hadn't kept tabs on her over the years. Otherwise he would have known about Sarge. "No, he retired three years ago."

"Really?" One of his dark eyebrows quirked up in surprise. "I can't imagine Sarge retired." At that moment his shovel hit something hard and metallic-sounding.

"Oh, my gosh. The treasure…it's really here." She sprang forward and peered into the hole he'd dug. Any anger or resentment she felt toward him was squashed beneath a rush of excitement.

"Hang on…move back…I'm not sure what I've hit. It could just be a rock."

But it wasn't a rock. She watched as he used the point of the shovel to dig around the object, which appeared to be an old tin box.

"I can't believe it's here," she said, watching as he scooted dirt from the surface and freed the edges. "I thought this was where the clues led, but I couldn't be sure."

He laid the shovel aside and reached into the hole to pull out the box. With a grunt, he freed it and stood. It was a plain gray tin box tied in the center with what looked as though it had once been a piece of lace.

"This doesn't look like it was buried a couple of weeks ago," he said, a frown marring his handsome, broad forehead.

"Open it!" she exclaimed eagerly. "We won't know if the money is inside unless you open it."

Suddenly her mind worked to process the fact that Joshua was back in town, that he looked as if he'd not only survived the years away, but had thrived. And he had her treasure...the money that had been going to change her life.

It wasn't fair. But if there was one thing Claire had learned in her twenty-six years on earth, it was that life wasn't fair and seemed to take particular pleasure in kicking her.

She watched as he attempted to untie the piece of lace. It disintegrated beneath his fingers and fell to the ground. Once again she took a step toward him and smelled the pleasant, spicy scent of his cologne. It was different from that he'd once worn.

When he'd left her five years before, for months she'd smelled the scent of him lingering on her skin, whispering in the air, taunting her with all that had been lost.

She shoved all thoughts of the past aside as his long, strong fingers worked to open the box. The box opened toward him, so she couldn't immediately see what was inside.

She watched his face as he peered inside, saw a look of bewilderment, then shock. "What...what is it?"

He looked at her, his green eyes filled with confusion. "I hate to burst your bubble, Cookie, but there's no money in here. There's just an old photograph."

"An old photograph?" Disappointment swept through her. "An old photograph of what?"

"I think you have to see it to believe it." He plucked the picture out of the box and held it out to her.

She took the photo and looked at it, for a moment not comprehending what she saw. It was obvious the picture was old; it was on faded paper in sepia tones.

It was a young couple, a formal sitting with the woman in a straight-backed chair and a man standing at her side. They wore clothing that dated the picture to the 1800s, but it was their faces that sent an electric shock through Claire.

The man was the spitting image of Joshua and the woman was a mirror image of herself. She looked back up at Joshua, the photo shaking in her trembling hands. "They look just like us. I mean, they look exactly like us. How…how is that possible?"

Joshua looked at the woman he had once loved to distraction, unsure what caused him more confusion, the fact that there was a picture of the two of them that had been buried in a tin box or that after all these years something about her still managed to touch him. She looked much the same as she had on the day he'd left, except perhaps more fragile. Like a thin wisp of smoke, she was slender enough that it appeared as if the slightest of breezes might blow her away.

Her hair was still the color of corn silk, long and surprisingly thick. He wondered if she still used the same strawberry-scented shampoo?

Her eyes were as he remembered them…dark-lashed and gray as turbulent skies. They hadn't always been that way…there had been a time when they'd been the color of passion, of dreams…of love.

"Joshua?"

Her irritated voice pulled him back from the past and he took the photo from her and looked at it once again. There was no mistake. The people in the photo were virtual clones of him and her.

"I don't know...I don't know how it's possible," he replied.

"But they look exactly like us," she repeated, a sense of wonder in her voice.

He turned the picture over. There was writing on the back, so faint it was almost illegible. He read aloud, "Daniel and Sarah Walker, 1856." He looked back at Claire. "It appears we have something of a mystery here."

For a moment, their gazes remained locked, and in the depths of her smoky eyes he saw bewilderment, wonder and something soft and yielding. It was there only a moment, then gone, as dark shutters snapped into place.

"*We* don't have anything," she replied. "You have an old photo and I have nothing." She turned to leave, stiffening as he fell into step beside her.

"Aren't you curious?" he asked, as they made their way back through the woods.

"Curious about what?"

He held the tin box out in front of her. "About them? About Daniel and Sarah, about why they look like us? Maybe they're long-lost relatives or, you know, what do you call them, doppelgängers."

He wanted to ask her if she'd felt it, the strange tingle and warmth that had raced up his arm when he'd first picked up the photo.

"The only thing I'm curious about is why

you're walking with me instead of going back to wherever you came from,'' she replied coolly.

As the path narrowed, he fell behind her. He dodged a sapling branch that nearly slapped him in the face as she passed by it. She still had the sexiest rear end he'd ever seen.

''I thought I'd stop in and say hello to Sarge,'' he replied and forced his gaze upward from her shapely derriere.

He could tell she didn't like the idea of him coming home with her by the way her shoulders stiffened and her strides grew faster.

He didn't try to speak to her again. There would come a time later when they would have to talk, when the past and the future would have to be laid to rest. But now was not the time. He knew he'd shocked her by his unexpected presence and she needed time to adjust. He needed time to adjust, as well.

He'd thought he would breeze into Mayfield, take care of his unfinished business, then walk away without a backward glance. He hadn't expected to feel a tug of crazy, mixed-up emotions when he saw her again.

When they hit the sidewalk outside City Hall, she continued to walk several paces in front of him, as if she didn't want anyone who might see them to know they were together.

He looked around as they headed down Main Street, again noting the changes that had taken place in the small town since he'd left. Stores he remembered were gone, replaced either by empty storefronts or new shops.

"It's funny, somehow everything looks smaller than I thought it was," he observed. He pointed down the road to where in the distance were the remains of an old, two-story home. "I see Hazel Benton's house burned."

"Yeah, a couple of years ago. Faulty wiring." She frowned, as if irritated that he'd forced her into talking.

"Remember when we were kids we all thought old Hazel was a witch and the rumor was that at night she wandered the streets of Mayfield looking for little children she could snatch and have for breakfast the next morning?"

"I remember," she said. A ghost of a smile curved her lips. It wasn't a real smile, but it was the closest thing he'd seen.

He suddenly wished for one of her smiles, the sound of her laughter. God, he'd always loved the sound of her laughter.

There had been a lot of laughter in the first two years of their marriage when they'd been too young, and perhaps too stupid to realize how life could take away all laughter if you allowed it.

Six years ago, he'd been a small-town boy in a small-town world married to the love of his life. In an instant of tragedy it had all been ripped apart.

But he wasn't here to pick over the carrion of what had once been.

As Sarge's house came into view, surprise swept through him at the unkempt condition. The lawn that had always been well-manicured now desperately needed a mowing, and the house itself begged for a new coat of paint. A piece of guttering dangled precariously from one corner of the roof.

"Looks like Sarge has let things go a little bit," he observed, quickening his footsteps once again to fall in beside her.

"You've been away a long time. Things have changed. Sarge has changed." Her voice held an edge sharp enough to slice steel.

Apparently some things hadn't changed...like the fact that she was still filled with a bitterness and rancor where he was concerned. When he told her he'd come back here for a divorce, he wondered if that would simply deepen her bitterness or finally set her free?

# Chapter Two

Joshua followed Claire up onto the front porch; he and Claire had spent many evenings on the swing that had once hung there. It had been on the swing that he had asked her to marry him. They'd been barely eighteen years old and she'd been three months pregnant.

As he followed her through the front door, the house greeted him with familiar smells... The scent of old wood and lemon polish, of sun-washed curtains and the faint odor of the menthol rub Sarge had always used on his bad shoulder.

He and Claire had spent the five years of their marriage here, beneath this roof. They'd been too young to afford their own place and Joshua had no real family of his own. From the time he'd been fifteen and had begun dating Claire, Claire and Sarge had become his family.

He tried to hide his surprise as Wilma Iverson, the next-door neighbor, came into the living room from the kitchen. Her faded blue eyes registered her own surprise at the sight of him. "Land's sakes, if it isn't Joshua McCane."

"Hello, Mrs. Iverson," he replied.

She snorted. "Ah, today it's Mrs. Iverson, but I still remember when you were nothing more than a snot-nosed kid and called me the battle-ax behind my back."

"Why, I don't remember any such thing," Joshua laughed in protest.

"Where's Sarge?" Claire asked.

Wilma nodded her head toward the hallway. "In his room, pouting."

Joshua saw the tension that tugged at Claire's delicate features. "What happened?" she asked.

"I caught him with a bag of candy and I took it away from him. I told him I wasn't going to be a party to him killing himself."

Joshua listened to all this with interest, wondering what Wilma was doing here and why she would take candy away from a grown man. An edge of disquiet surged up inside him.

"Sarge!" Claire yelled down the hallway. "Come on out. There's somebody here to see you."

"If it's that creature from next door, I'm not

coming out,'' Sarge's voice rang out, the strength in the tone soothing Joshua's momentary alarm. Claire winced and offered a look of apology at Wilma.

"It's not me. I'm leaving, you old coot,'' she yelled down the hallway. She smiled at Claire and Joshua, then headed toward the door. "Let me know if you need me again, dear. You know where to find me.''

As she went out the front door, Joshua heard a bump, a resounding curse, then a strange whirring noise. He looked down the hallway, shock rocking him as he saw the frail, white-haired man in a motorized wheelchair making his way slowly down the hall.

Sarge. He appeared to have aged fifty years in the last five. He stopped short of the living room and turned his head from side to side. "Claire?''

It was at that moment Joshua realized that Sarge was not only thin and frail, but blind, as well. He shot a quick glance at Claire, wanting to know what had happened to the vital, strong man Joshua had loved like a father. But of course, she couldn't answer his unspoken questions. Not here...not now.

"Hello, Sarge,'' Joshua said.

The old man's face lit with obvious pleasure and he gasped in surprise. "Well, I'll be damned. Come closer, Joshua boy, so I can smell the rascal and know it's really you.''

Joshua laughed and walked over to Sarge's chair, then leaned down and gave the old man a hug, his heart aching as he felt Sarge's thinness. He didn't miss the fact that Sarge's arms didn't raise to return the hug.

"Ah, don't smell no rascal, only smell fancy cologne and grown-up man."

Joshua laughed again. "There's a little rascal left," he replied.

"Cookie, put some coffee on, me and the boy got some catching up to do. Joshua, wheel me into the kitchen. They got me this damned fool chair with a motor, but it just makes me run into things at a faster speed."

Joshua set the tin box they'd dug up on the coffee table, then moved behind the chair and pushed Sarge toward the kitchen. Claire walked in front of him and he knew by the straight set of her shoulders that she didn't intend to be a welcoming hostess.

The kitchen was just as Joshua remembered it, a large airy space with floor-to-ceiling windows that faced the east. Many a morning he and Sarge had drunk coffee while morning light filtered in through the windows.

There was no chair in the place at the table where Sarge had always sat, and it was here that Joshua pushed him up against the table.

Joshua took the chair across from Sarge as Claire busied herself making a pot of coffee. Samuel Cook, 'Sarge' as he had been known for as long as Joshua could remember, had been a robust, strong man who had looked and acted half his age when Joshua had left Mayfield.

Regret swept through him as he gazed at what Sarge had become. He wasn't sure what had put the old man in the wheelchair and stolen his sight, but he felt he never should have stayed away for so long.

"You still making a killing with those games of yours?" Sarge asked.

"Yeah, business is booming and the games are doing better than I ever dreamed." Joshua's gaze slid to Claire, who had her back to them. Her long hair rippled down to the center of her back, sparked by the sunshine dancing in through the windows.

"Who'd have thought it, that a grown man could spend his time playing games and make a fortune." Sarge shook his head. "In my day, kids didn't have Play Stations and Nintendos to pass the time."

"It's a different generation, Sarge," Joshua replied. It was still hard for Joshua to believe that he'd managed to parlay the fantasy stories he'd made up to sustain himself through a tough childhood into a financial empire of sorts.

Just a month earlier, *Business* magazine had done an article on him and his company. The article had been entitled, "Joshua McCane: The Man

Behind the Magic," and had chronicled his mete-
oric career from his first little company, begun in
a rented space above a health-food store four years
ago.

DreamQuest Games now had its own building
on twenty-five beautiful acres in California. Joshua
employed two hundred men and women who
worked at producing and marketing the fantasy
games both children and young adults had em-
braced.

He glanced at Claire, surprised to see her staring
at him. As their gazes met, she quickly looked
away and grabbed the sugar bowl and creamer for
the table.

"Mind if I wash up? My hands are dirty." Without waiting for her reply, he stood and walked over
to the sink.

Claire moved aside, but not before he smelled
the floral scent of her perfume.

The scent had a touch of honeysuckle to it. Instantly he remembered those summer nights when
he and Claire had made out on the porch swing
with the sweet scent of the nearby honeysuckle
wafting in the air.

"When did you get into town?" Sarge asked, as
Joshua turned on the faucet and shoved those
memories aside.

"Late last night. I ran into Claire this morning
out by the old Dragon Tree." He finished washing
his hands and turned off the water.

"Were you out there digging for the ten thousand bucks, too?" Sarge asked.

Joshua took the hand towel Claire proffered and dried his hands. Her gaze was cool, disinterested, but as she took the towel back from him he noticed that her hand trembled slightly. So, she wasn't as unaffected by his presence as she wanted him to believe.

He sat back down at the table. "I was drinking a cup of coffee this morning at the diner and reading the paper. I saw the clues for the treasure hunt, and you know I've never been able to resist a puzzle."

"I guess Cookie didn't find the treasure, otherwise she wouldn't be pouting now," Sarge said.

"I'm not pouting," Claire stated as she poured three cups of coffee. "I'm just listening." She set one of the cups of coffee in front of Sarge. "Twelve o'clock," she murmured. "And no, I didn't find the money. All we found was an old tin box."

"With a photo inside," Joshua added. "An old photo of a couple who look exactly like Claire and me." He took a mug of coffee from her, surprised that as their fingers touched he felt a responding surge of heat sweep up his arm.

She jerked her hand back as if she felt it too and the scowl on her beautiful features deepened.

"Well, that's strange," Sarge exclaimed. "You say the people in it look like you and Claire?"

"They could be our twins," Joshua replied. The photo in the old tin box wasn't the only thing strange around here, he thought.

He wanted to know what had caused Sarge's blindness and his descent into a wheelchair. How long had Sarge been sick, and had Claire been dealing with it all on her own? He wanted to know when things had gotten so obviously bad.

What he found stranger than anything was that the woman he'd finally come here to divorce still had the ability to fill him with a white-hot desire and a deep yearning for something he couldn't identify.

"How long are you staying?" Sarge asked as he carefully brought his cup to his lips to sip the fresh brew.

"I'm not sure." Joshua leaned back in the chair, his gaze once again falling on Claire.

He's leaving as soon as he finishes his cup of coffee, Claire wanted to say. He's getting back on whatever plane or train or bus brought him here, and he's never coming back again.

He smiled at her, as if he read her thoughts, then directed his attention back to Sarge. "I don't have any definite schedule. I just decided I needed a little time away from work. You know what they say about all work and no play."

"Damned right," Sarge exclaimed. "Making

money is nice, but there's other things important in life, too. You'll stay here,'' Sarge added firmly.

"Oh, I don't…'' Joshua began.

"I'm sure Joshua will be more comfortable at the Red Inn,'' Claire interjected quickly. She assumed he was at the Red Inn since it was the only motel in town.

"Nonsense,'' Sarge replied. "I've been trying to get both the Health Department and the Building Codes people to shut that place down for years. It's not fit for a skunk. You're family, Joshua. You'll stay here and that's final. Now, tell me all about this business of yours and about all the loony people in California. I hear tell the women sunbathe stark-naked there.''

Claire didn't want to listen to Joshua extol the luxurious lifestyle he'd built for himself, nor did she like the way his very presence stirred not only memories of what had once been, but also an edge of physical awareness that was distinctly uncomfortable.

She excused herself from the table and left the kitchen. She wandered back into the living room, drawn to the tin box Joshua had left on the coffee table. She sat on the sofa and pulled the box onto her lap.

Her fingers trembled slightly as she opened it and picked up the picture. Immediately, a strange electrical surge washed up her arm. It wasn't unpleasant, just warm and disconcerting. She'd felt it when she'd first taken the picture from Joshua.

She dismissed the sensation, telling herself she was out of sorts, highly on edge and that's why she thought she felt something strange.

Again she studied the features of the two people in the photo. There was no question about it. They shared more than a passing resemblance to her and Joshua. It was as if she and Joshua had sat for the photo in one of those vacation photo places where you could dress up in historical outfits.

But they had never had a photo like this taken and there seemed to be no explanation as to why Sarah and Daniel Walker looked exactly like Claire and Joshua McCane.

The couple in the picture wasn't smiling, nor did there seem to be any hint of intimacy between them. He stared straight ahead, one of his hands resting not on her shoulder, but rather on the top of the chair where she sat.

She thought she detected a weary sadness about them, especially radiating from Sarah's eyes. Who were these people and why had they buried a photo of themselves in the middle of nowhere?

She placed the photo back in the box, disturbed by it more than she cared to admit.

"Sarge would like you to take him back to his room for a nap."

She started at the sound of Joshua's voice coming from the kitchen doorway. Fighting against a burst of weariness that had become as familiar as the color of her own eyes in the mirror, she rose from the sofa.

"He usually gets quite tired at this time of the day," she said unnecessarily.

He stepped out of the doorway and into the living room. "I'll just wait here. We need to talk."

"It usually takes me a while to get him settled in." She hoped he'd get the hint, that he'd realize they had nothing to talk about, that she had nothing to discuss with him.

"I'll wait." He sank onto the sofa where she had been seated only moments before, looking for all the world as if he had a right to be there.

It took her nearly twenty minutes to get Sarge into bed and settled comfortably. As always, seeing him so thin and helpless against the sheets nearly broke what was left of her heart.

Sarge was all the family she'd ever had. He'd raised her since she was eight, when her parents had been killed in a car accident. She loved him as fiercely as she'd ever loved anyone in her life. "You rest easy," she said softly, then left his bedroom.

When she returned to the living room, Joshua was still seated on the sofa. He rose when she entered the room. "You want to tell me what's going on around here? What happened to Sarge?"

She raised a finger to her lips and indicated he should follow her out the front door. When they were both on the porch, she turned to him. Maybe if she answered his questions he would go away.

"Three years ago, Sarge began to complain about his eyesight, but you know how he's always been about going to doctors."

"Yeah, wild horses couldn't drag him." He leaned a hip against the porch railing and for the first time she noticed the small differences time had wrought in him. He'd been recklessly handsome at eighteen, dangerously attractive at twenty.

But now, at twenty-five, tiny lines had appeared, fanning out from his startling green eyes, and there was a sheen of worldliness about him that merely added to his physical appeal.

"Anyway, I didn't realize just how bad it was until he wrecked his police car." She looked out toward the yard, finding it easier to speak if she wasn't looking at him.

"The accident wasn't a bad one, but it convinced him he needed to see a doctor. We discovered he had diabetes, probably had had it for years and the degeneration in his eyes was massive."

"Is there anything they can do? Any kind of operation?" he asked.

She shook her head, still keeping her gaze focused in the distance. "He's had two operations on his eyes, but they were unsuccessful. Anyway, over the last two years he's adjusted fairly well to the blindness. Then, last month he had a stroke. That's what put him in the wheelchair and he hasn't been dealing very well with the new challenges.''

She didn't even realize Joshua had moved from his position until his hand closed around her forearm. ''Why didn't you contact me and tell me what was going on?'' His green eyes held the first stir of anger. ''I had a right to know that he was ill.''

She jerked her arm away from his grasp and took a step back from him. You had no right. You lost your rights when you walked out, she wanted to say, but she didn't. ''There was nothing you could do...nothing anyone could do. Besides, I'm handling things.''

''Handling things?'' He gestured toward the yard. ''That's certainly not the way I see it. It looks like everything is falling apart around you.''

''That's not true,'' she protested. ''I've just...just gotten a little behind with things.''

He studied her for a long moment. ''You look tired, Claire, and you're too thin. Who is helping you care for Sarge?''

''I don't need help taking care of him. I told you, we're fine.'' She raised her chin and for a moment their gazes remained locked. ''I know Sarge issued an invitation for you to stay here, but I really think you'd be more comfortable at the motel.''

His eyes lightened in hue and a smile curved the corners of his lips. ''Why, Cookie, you're almost making me think you don't want me here.''

"I don't want you here. This is Sarge's house…my home, and you chose to leave it a long time ago."

"You made it impossible for me to stay," he replied, the light in his eyes diminishing. "But I have no intention of rehashing the past." He shoved his hands into his pockets. "However, you're mistaken about one thing. Two years ago I paid off the mortgage on this house, and Sarge insisted I put it in my name. So, I'm really not intruding in your house, for the past two years, I've allowed you to live in mine."

This was the second shock of the day, and Claire wondered how many of these she could take without having a breakdown of some sort. "Then, I guess I have no say as to whether you stay here or not," she finally said, hoping her voice resonated with a nonchalance she didn't feel.

"Claire." He pulled his hands from his pockets and took a step toward her. "Contrary to what you seem to believe, I'm not here to cause you grief. I'd say five years ago we pretty much exhausted that particular emotion."

He drew a deep breath and looked away from her. "I'd like to spend some time with Sarge, and at least for the short period of time that I'm here, I could help you out a little. You know, maybe mow the lawn and do a little yard clean-up."

"The spare bedroom is made up," she finally said, knowing that she was being selfish in not wanting him here. Sarge would enjoy his company and that should be all that was important. Surely she could handle his presence here for a few days as long as he didn't intend to talk about the past.

"I've got some things to do this afternoon. Why don't I come back here with my things after dinner, say about seven."

"That will be fine," she replied, weary resignation sweeping through her.

He turned to leave, but paused and turned back to face her. "Claire, it is good to see you again." He didn't wait for her to reply, but instead turned once again and left, walking briskly down the sidewalk.

She sank down on the steps, watching until he was out of sight.

Joshua.

He'd been a teenager from the wrong side of the tracks, raised by an alcoholic uncle and she'd been the sheriff's granddaughter. They'd been fifteen when he'd first asked her out and on that very first date she fell hopelessly, helplessly in love with him.

She'd spent the last five years of her existence trying to forget him and everything that had happened in that last year of their marriage.

She stood and brushed off the seat of her pants, hoping he didn't intend to stay too long. One thing was certain, while he was here, she would keep her distance, both physically and emotionally.

She couldn't go back to that place in time, couldn't dwell in ancient memories. She feared that if she did, she would lose her mind to the grief and never surface again.

# Chapter Three

It was just after seven when Joshua returned to the house. He carried with him a large suitcase of clothing and his state-of-the-art laptop computer.

He was tired. He'd been tired for the last year. From the moment he'd left here five years earlier, he'd thrown himself into work, as if achieving success would banish his heartache. He'd worked long hours, seven days a week to make something of himself, to fill the lonely hours that would otherwise be painfully empty.

He wasn't sure whether it was his success or merely the passing of time that had finally healed some of the grief he'd left here with, but he no longer felt crippled by the weight of what had been lost.

In fact, it was time to move on and that's what had brought him back here. He had to resolve the past before he could forge ahead with his future.

Claire opened the door before he could knock, obviously expecting him. Gone was the anger and resentment that had sparked in her eyes earlier in the day. Apparently, she had resigned herself to him being here.

"Come on in," she said and opened the door wider to allow him entry.

"Thanks." He maneuvered through the door and dropped his suitcase just inside.

"Hey, Joshua, get your things stored away and come watch this quiz show with me," Sarge said from his wheelchair in front of the television. "I want to see if I can still whip your butt at answering the questions."

Joshua laughed. "Okay, just let me get settled in." He turned to Claire. "Sit down and relax. I know the way to the spare room." He picked up his suitcase and headed down the hallway.

The first door on the left was Sarge's bedroom. The first on the right was the room that he and Claire had shared during their marriage. The second door on the left was the bathroom and the last door on the right was the spare room.

As he approached the room where he would be staying, an unexpected knot of tension balled up in the pit of his stomach.

The door was closed and he hesitated a moment,

his hand on the knob. The last time he'd been in the room, there had been blue curtains at the window and a teddy-bear wallpaper border around the ceiling.

The room had smelled of little boy and been filled with all of Joshua's dreams, his hopes, his love.

Drawing a deep breath, he turned the knob and opened the door. White lacy curtains billowed at the window, bringing the scent of summer into the room. Pale-yellow walls matched the sunflower designs on the bedspread and accentuated the white wicker furniture.

There was no hint of baby's-breath-and-powder scent, no lingering reminder of the beloved child who had once slept here, played here.

He placed his suitcase and laptop next to the single bed, almost able to hear the childish giggles that had once filled this space.

Baby Sammy. Named after Sarge, Claire and Joshua's son had become the center of the universe on the day he'd been born. With Joshua's dark hair and Claire's smoky eyes, he'd been a little charmer with a ready smile and an easy disposition.

I miss you, Sammy, he thought. He missed Sammy and Claire and Sarge and the way things had been a long time ago.

''I just remembered that you like extra pillows.''

He whirled around to see Claire standing in the

doorway, two pillows clutched to her chest. She held them out to him.

"Yeah…thanks." He took the pillows and tossed them on the bed, then walked to the window and peered out onto a backyard as tangled and overgrown as the front. "Do you have a lawn mower that works?" he asked and turned back to look at her.

She crossed her arms over her chest. "You didn't come back here to mow the lawn."

He smiled. "True, but if you remember, I used to enjoy yard work. I don't mind doing it, really. I spend most of the hours of my day sitting at a desk. The physical activity will be good for me."

She uncrossed her arms and offered him a tentative smile. "Lately there just haven't seemed to be enough hours in the day to get everything done. Sarge doesn't like to be alone and he's been so cantankerous it's been hard to get people to sit with him."

"Claire?" As if to prove her point, Sarge's voice rang out.

"We're coming," she answered and together the two of them left the bedroom and returned to the living room. Joshua sat on the sofa, vaguely disappointed when Claire sat across the room in a chair instead of on the sofa with him. He wouldn't have minded if she'd sat close enough for him to smell her sweet fragrance.

The evening passed quickly. Although Sarge

couldn't see, his mind was sharp as a tack and he and Joshua battled each other answering questions on first one game show, then another.

During the commercials, they chatted and it didn't take long for Joshua to get a picture of what life had been like for these two during the past three years. Since Sarge's blindness, Claire's sole job was taking care of Sarge, and Joshua had a feeling there had been little time for leisure or fun in Claire's life.

It was also apparent from several things that Sarge said that money was always an issue, that between his small monthly checks and his medical needs, there was never any money for little extras.

If only Claire had cashed the checks he'd mailed to her, surely the extra money would have come in handy. But he knew why she hadn't. Claire had a healthy dose of pride; couple that with the hatred of him she'd professed when he'd left, and he'd never really been surprised that she'd refused any money he'd sent her.

It was just after nine when Sarge fell asleep in his chair and Claire said she needed to put him to bed. She wheeled him down the hallway and disappeared into his bedroom. Joshua waited a couple of minutes, then walked down the hallway.

When he looked into the bedroom, he saw Claire struggling to get Sarge from the wheelchair onto the bed. She'd already managed to take off the old man's shoes and socks.

"Come on, Sarge, you've got to help me here," she murmured, her arms wrapped around the man's chest.

Joshua didn't hesitate. He gently moved her aside, then leaned down and scooped the thin man up in his arms and placed him on the bed. Sarge mumbled something incoherently in his sleep, then turned his head and began to snore.

"Thanks," she murmured, although her voice held no gratitude, but rather an edge of resentment.

He nodded curtly. "You want him undressed?"

"No, he'll be fine for the night. In the morning I'll help him change his clothes." She covered the sleeping man with a sheet, then she and Joshua left the bedroom.

"Would you come sit on the porch with me?" he asked. "It's a beautiful night and I'd like to talk to you."

She frowned. "I'm really tired, and Sarge gets up early in the mornings. Besides, if you want to talk to me you can do it right here."

He eyed her with a small smile. "What's the matter, Cookie? Afraid to sit with me in the dark?"

She rose to his bait, a flush of color staining her cheeks. "Just for a minute," she said and swept past him and out the front door.

He followed behind her and together they sank down on the top step with inches between them. For a moment neither of them spoke. Nighttime in Mayfield was always quiet, peaceful.

There were no sirens in the distance, no traffic noises to disrupt the rhythmic cadence of the insects that filled the air. The sky overhead was a blanket of stars and a plump near-full moon hung suspended in the air as if by magic. "There's nothing prettier than a Mayfield moon," he observed.

"It's the same moon that shines in California," she replied.

He laughed lightly. "I suppose it is. It just looks prettier from here."

She released a sigh that whispered of exhaustion, and he turned to look at her, noting how the moonlight bathed her beautiful features in a silvery glow.

"How long do you think you can keep this up?" he asked softly.

She didn't pretend not to know what he was talking about. "As long as it's necessary." She sighed again. "You've just caught us at a bad time. Things will get better. The doctor expects Sarge to be able to get out of the wheelchair with some physical therapy and time."

"So, he isn't paralyzed?"

"No, just weak."

"Is he seeing a physical therapist?"

She hesitated a moment, then shook her head. "Not right now. He's being difficult and wallowing in pity. But with a little more time that will change."

"Claire, given a little more time, you're going

to end up in the hospital with a bad case of exhaustion. You need to hire some help.''

''That kind of help doesn't come cheap.'' She said the words with great reluctance. ''And don't even offer because I don't want a dime from you. Sarge and I can handle things just fine on our own.''

A stir of anger rose up inside him. ''Dammit, Claire, your stubborn self-reliance is someday going to be the death of you.'' It had already been the death of their marriage. The words rang in his head, but he bit them back before they could be spoken aloud. Nothing could be served by going back to that place in time.

''If you brought me out here to extol my character flaws, then I think this conversation is finished.'' She started to rise, but he grabbed her hand and pulled her back down next to him.

''Wait…okay, I'm sorry,'' he exclaimed. She pulled her hand from his and remained tensed as if for flight. Once again, he became aware of her fresh-scented perfume and the heat of her body and he fought a sudden desire to reach out and pull her into his arms.

However, with far too much clarity he remembered how stiff and unyielding her body had been the last time he'd attempted to hold her.

''What are you going to do with the treasure if you find it?'' he asked.

She eyed him, her gray eyes almost silver in the

moonlight. "I don't know, maybe hire the help that you think I need. We don't need anyone full-time, just maybe a day or two a week so I can get a part-time job and help out with the bills." She reached a hand up and touched a length of her hair.

"And if there's anything left over, maybe go to the beauty shop and have your hair and nails done?" He smiled at her look of surprise. "I haven't forgotten how much you used to enjoy a trip to Betty's Beauty Spa."

A tiny smile whispered at her lips. "I can't remember the last time somebody else washed my hair for me." The smile disappeared. "I still don't understand what you wanted to talk to me about."

"I have a deal to offer you."

"What kind of a deal?"

"I'll help you find that treasure while I'm here, if in return you help me find out something about Daniel and Sarah Walker." It had been an idea that had been boiling around in his head all evening. He knew Claire would never take anything from him, but hoped she'd let him help her get at least some of the money they so obviously needed.

"How am I supposed to find out anything about those people?" she asked.

He shrugged. "Mayfield was begun in 1849. Maybe they were citizens. You used to like digging around in the old records at City Hall."

"I don't have the time," she exclaimed.

"You could take the time while I'm here," he

countered. "I can entertain Sarge and give you the time to take a break from here and see what you can find."

She frowned, obviously thinking about it. "They can't be long-lost relatives of mine. I did our genealogy a long time ago and I don't recall any Walkers in the family tree." She swirled a strand of her hair between two fingers and he wished it were his fingers touching the silk of her hair. "Why do you care about those people in the picture anyway?"

"Aside from the fact that they look just like us?" He stared up at the moon, trying to find the words to explain to her what he'd felt from the moment he'd seen that photo.

He looked back at her, wondering if she'd think he'd lost his mind. "I just feel as though fate put that picture there in the ground for us to find, that we were meant to find it for a reason."

She stood and brushed off the seat of her shorts. "And I'd say fate already had its go at us and I have no intention of letting it dabble in my life ever again."

She moved to the front door. "But I'll take you up on that deal. You help me find the treasure money and I'll see what I can find out about Sarah and Daniel Walker for you. With any luck, both can be accomplished very quickly." With these last words she disappeared back into the house.

Joshua remained where he was seated. He tipped

his head back and once again stared up at the moon, as the sound of the night insects created a lullaby.

He'd come here with every intention of cutting ties with Claire. He'd come to tell her he was finally going to get a divorce from her, but finding that picture had thrown him for a loop.

He hadn't been kidding when he'd told her that he felt as though fate was at work here. What were the odds that it would be he and Claire who would dig up that old picture? And why on earth did the two people in the photo look exactly like them?

Sighing, he rose from the stoop. For the moment he wasn't going to mention a divorce to Claire. He was going to wait and see what they could find out about the couple in the photo.

He was going to wait and see if fate intended to be kind or if it merely intended to kick them in the teeth once again.

Claire stood at the kitchen window, sipping coffee and watching Joshua as he pushed the lawn mower across the expanse of the backyard. The whir of the motor roared through the open window, bringing with it the pleasant scent of freshly mowed grass.

Sarge sat at the table behind her, eating his breakfast of oatmeal, the clank of his spoon against the bowl barely penetrating Claire's concentration.

Joshua's broad bare chest gleamed in the morning sunshine and his jean shorts emphasized his slim waist and hips and the length of his long, muscular legs. Had his chest always been so impossibly broad? Had his back always been so filled with strength?

As she watched him efficiently transforming the area from a wild tangle to a neatly trimmed yard, she felt a curl of heat unfurl in the pit of her stomach.

All too vividly she could remember how that broad chest felt against her naked breasts, how the scent of his skin would linger on her own long after they'd finished making love.

All too painfully she could remember how eager she would be during the day for night to come, knowing that in the darkness of the night they would make love and talk about dreams and eventually fall asleep in each other's arms.

She still couldn't believe he was here. In the five years that he'd been gone he'd written fairly often, and in each of those letters she'd expected him to tell her he wanted a divorce, but the letters had never indicated anything about the status of their marriage.

Was that why he'd returned? Was he here to tell her he was finally going to sever the last of his ties with her? He was a good-looking man in his prime. Had he fallen in love with another woman? Was he ready to begin again, to marry and have a family and live happily ever after?

CARLA CASSIDY                    49

She'd been expecting it, so why did the thought of him making a life with another woman fill her with a small surge of jealousy and a touch of regret?

"He's a good man, Cookie." Sarge's voice pulled her from her thoughts and she turned away from the window.

"I suppose." She moved to the counter to pour herself some more coffee. "Why didn't you tell me he paid off the mortgage on the house two years ago?"

Sarge backed his wheelchair several inches away from the table, indicating that he was finished with his breakfast. "Because I knew it wouldn't sit right with you, not that it was any of your business anyway. He paid the mortgage and the house is now in his name and yours."

"Mine?" She eyed her grandfather in surprise. Joshua hadn't mentioned that little fact when he'd told her she'd been living in his house for the past two years.

"This place is all I had that was worth anything. I was going to put it in your names anyway. You and Joshua can fight it out after I'm gone."

"What is it we're going to fight about?" Joshua asked as he entered the back door. Instantly Claire felt as if he filled every corner of the kitchen with his masculine scent and half-naked body. She was struck with a flare of desire so intense it cramped her stomach.

"Nothing. We aren't going to fight about anything," she replied quickly and moved to take Sarge's bowl off the table.

"Good." He walked over to the sink and reached in the cabinet for a glass. "It's far too pretty out today to fight with anyone."

Claire watched as he filled a glass with water then brought it to his lips. He drank deeply, a droplet of water falling from the bottom of the glass and landing in the center of his chest.

Her head suddenly filled with the memory of a dream she'd had the night before, a dream about Sarah and Daniel Walker. In her dream they had stood by the edge of a creek, and Daniel had bent down and scooped up a handful of the crisp, clean water. He'd raised his hands to his mouth and droplets of the liquid had escaped and fallen on his beautiful chest.

He'd grinned at Sarah, his eyes filled with a love so intense that it had ached in Claire's heart when she'd awakened that morning.

"Hello? Anybody home?" Joshua said.

The image of Daniel and Sarah disappeared and she stared at Joshua blankly. "Excuse me?"

"I said it's such a beautiful day why don't we do a picnic lunch and take it out to Miller's Park? We can take all the clues to the treasure hunt and brainstorm in the fresh air and sunshine."

"You kids go ahead," Sarge said. "It's too much trouble to get me and my chair out for a picnic. I'll be fine here alone for a couple of hours.''

Claire was unsurprised by Sarge's words. She'd been unable to get him out anywhere since he'd had his stroke.

''Oh, no, you don't,'' Joshua exclaimed. He set his glass in the sink. ''You aren't weaseling out of this. If you don't go, then Cookie and I won't go.'' He winked at Claire. ''And I can tell by the look on Cookie's face that she really wants to go on a picnic, and you know how she pouts when she doesn't get her way.''

A burst of laughter exploded out of Claire at his audacity. Joshua smiled at her and for a moment in the depths of his spring-green eyes she saw a glimpse of what had once been. Desire, rich and bold spilled from the green depths of his gaze.

She broke the eye contact, disturbed that what she felt was a deep wistfulness, a yearning for something that had never been…would never be.

''I reckon we don't want Cookie pouting, so I guess we'll have a picnic,'' Sarge finally replied. ''Besides, it will be kind of like old times, won't it? We had some fine times in the past picnicking out at Miller's Park.''

Claire felt Joshua looking at her once again, but she refused to meet his gaze. ''Yeah, we did,'' he agreed softly.

''Why don't I finish mowing the front lawn and

Claire can pack a lunch, then we'll take off around noon.''

''Sounds like a plan,'' Sarge replied.

Claire supposed she should be grateful that Joshua had managed to get Sarge to agree to an outing. It would be good for Sarge to get out of the house for a few hours. And she *was* grateful, but that gratefulness was tinged with a dark uneasiness as she thought of the planned picnic.

Sarge was right, some of the best times of their life together as a family had been spent on summer-day picnics at Miller's Park. But she didn't want to remember that happy time in her life and she didn't want to think of the emotion she'd thought she'd seen momentarily shining in Joshua's eyes, an emotion that looked surprisingly like desire.

If Joshua had come back here to ask her for a divorce, then something inside her would be broken forever. But if he'd come back here seeking some sort of reconciliation, then he'd be disappointed.

There was no way she could go back, no way she could allow herself to fall back into loving Joshua again.

## Chapter Four

Miller's Park was a favorite place for families to while away the lazy days of summer, especially on Saturdays and Sundays when the children were out of school.

This Sunday was no different. By the time they arrived at the park the playground was already filled with children. Mothers sat on the benches nearby, reading books or crocheting, looking up often to check on their offspring.

Claire chose the picnic site farthest away from the playground and Joshua wondered if she'd done it on purpose. As he carried Sarge's wheelchair to a spot beneath a shady oak tree, he thought of Sammy.

If an undetected heart defect hadn't taken him when he'd been almost two, he would have been nearly seven now. Joshua and Claire would have come here often to watch him climb the jungle gym or slip down the slide.

He unfolded the chair, then went back to the car for Sarge, shoving away the thoughts of what might have been. As Joshua carried Sarge, Claire grabbed the blanket and the picnic basket and followed just behind him.

"It will be good for Cookie to get out and spend a little time relaxing," Sarge said, as Joshua set him in his chair. "I'm afraid I'm a terrible burden on her."

"She doesn't look too much the worse for the wear," Joshua replied.

"Would you two stop talking about me as if I'm not here?" Claire exclaimed as she flopped down in the center of the blanket she'd spread out.

"She might not look stressed, but listen to her, she's stressed," Sarge exclaimed and winked one sightless eye in Joshua's direction.

"Ha-ha, you're very funny," Claire replied dryly. "And now, the big question of the day is, do we want to eat, then brainstorm on where the treasure might be, or brainstorm, then eat?"

"Definitely eat first," Joshua said as he joined her on the blanket. "I always think better on a full stomach."

"Me, too," Sarge quipped. He raised his face upward and sighed in what appeared to be peaceful contentment.

Joshua turned his attention to Claire, who was busy pulling items from the picnic basket. She had changed clothes for their outing and was now clad in a yellow tank top and shorts.

She'd been wearing yellow the first time he'd seen her, when they'd both been fifteen years old. And she'd been wearing yellow on the day he'd left her, a canary-yellow sweater and slacks that were in stark contrast to the darkness in her eyes.

As they ate lunch, Sarge chatted about the changes the past five years had brought to the small town. He seemed to know who had married whom, who had divorced, who got liquored up on Saturday nights and the issues that were facing the town council.

Joshua's attention was torn between trying to concentrate on what Sarge was saying and watching Claire eat. He'd noted that she had eaten hardly any of the breakfast she'd cooked that morning, her attention focused on making sure Sarge had what he needed. She looked as if she'd missed far too many meals in recent weeks.

She attacked the picnic fare with abandon, smiling sheepishly as he caught her licking her fingers. "Fresh air definitely does something wicked to my appetite," she exclaimed.

"It's good to see you enjoying yourself," he replied. "A few extra pounds certainly wouldn't hurt you."

"If that's the case, then how about you split the extra sandwich with me."

He smiled. "You go ahead. I'm stuffed."

When they'd finished with the meal and had repacked the basket, Sarge moved his wheelchair out of the shade and into the sun and promptly fell asleep.

"Thank you for getting him out today," Claire said, her gray eyes filled with a grudging gratitude. "He needs to get out more, work at getting his strength back, but he's so darned stubborn with me."

"He's probably angry, depressed...afraid."

She nodded and pulled her knees up to her chest, wrapping her arms around them. "All of the above, but he won't listen to me and he refuses to do anything to help himself. Of course, I'm not complaining about having to take care of him or anything like that," she hurriedly added.

"I didn't think you were," he assured her.

She studied him for a long moment. A breeze caressed her hair, sending a strand of it flying outward. He fought the impulse to reach out and capture the shiny silk between his fingers.

"How on earth did you get into video games, Joshua?" she asked. "I didn't even know you knew how to turn on a computer when you left here.''

He smiled. ''I didn't.'' He stretched out on his side, close enough to her that he could smell her sweet scent. ''When I left here, you know I had no real skills and no education.'' During the course of their marriage, he had worked pumping gas, sacking groceries, on heavy construction, whatever it took to support Claire and Sammy.

''Anyway, I knew if I was going to make something of myself I needed to learn a skill, so I took out a loan and enrolled in computer programming. To my surprise, it was something I excelled at. When I graduated from the school, I had a dozen offers with companies for more money than I'd ever dreamed of making, but I had a dream of owning my own company.''

He sat up and leaned his back against the trunk of the tree that provided the shade where they sat. ''Anyway, I took out more loans, started DreamQuest and nobody was more surprised than me when the games started taking off.''

''What kind of games are they?'' she asked.

''Mostly adventure. Remember those stories I used to tell you when we were younger?''

She smiled, the first real uncomplicated smile he'd seen since he'd arrived. It lit up her features with a warmth that spilled over him, and he wished he could capture it. ''You mean, those stories about lonely Lonnie looking for his parents and having to face the perils of the city all alone?''

He laughed. ''Exactly. Little Lonnie now has three games of his own and they're my top sellers. But there are also games about Mr. Blue, a crayon who doesn't want to be blue anymore, a carrot named Raymond who is trying to stay out of the clutches of a hungry rabbit and a lot more. And speaking of games, we're supposed to be brainstorming to find that treasure for you,'' he reminded her.

''Right.'' She opened the picnic basket and pulled out a notebook. ''I've got all the clues that have come out so far written down here, along with the places I've already looked for the money.'' She stretched out on her stomach, the notebook opened on the ground in front of her.

Joshua lay down next to her, also on his belly. He was careful to keep an inch or two between their bodies, knowing he no longer had the right to lie intimately close to her.

Still, he was close enough to feel her body heat, to inhale her scent surrounding him and the combination of the two created a ball of familiar tension in the pit of his stomach.

It was the same kind of aching need he'd always felt for her, and it stunned him to realize she still had the power to make him ache for her.

''The first clue that appeared in the paper was,

'With a scream like a banshee, the sound rides the wind. With this clue in mind, let the contest begin.'"

She turned her head to look at him. She was so close he could see the metal-gray flecks in her eyes, the small spattering of freckles across her nose. If he leaned forward just an inch, he would be able to capture her lips with his.

"Joshua?"

"Yeah, I'm thinking," he replied and tried to focus on the task at hand instead of the memory of how sweet and yielding her lips had once been beneath his. "Remind me of the second clue, maybe something will click in my head if I hear all the clues together." He stared down at the blanket beneath them, attempting to concentrate on what she was saying.

"The second clue was, 'Red is the color of my true love's hair. If you figure this out, the money is there.' And the last one was, 'The roots of fire and ash yield sweet fruit. If you find this place, you've got the loot.'"

He shot her a quick glance and saw her chewing on her bottom lip, a habit of hers when she was in deep concentration. "That's the one that made me go out to the Dragon Tree yesterday morning," he said.

She nodded. "Me, too. I remember how the kids used to talk about how the wind whistled through the leaves and I figured maybe it sounded like a banshee.''

''And the leaves turn bright red in the autumn, so that would fit with the second clue.'' He smiled at her. ''The Dragon Tree was a smart guess.''

''Yeah, unfortunately it was wrong,'' she replied wryly. She shifted positions and her thigh made contact with his. She quickly moved to break the contact, but not before he saw the slight flush that reddened her cheeks. She rolled away from him and onto her back, putting several additional inches between them. ''So, any other ideas?'' she asked.

He had other ideas all right. He had the idea to lean over her and capture her rosy lips with his own. His fingers itched with the idea of tangling in her hair or cupping the warmth of her breasts. He entertained the idea of kissing her, touching her, caressing her until her soft gray eyes darkened to the dark smoke of passion.

Desire, rich and hot, flooded through him, creating an ache deep within that he hadn't experienced in years. It shocked him and threw him mentally off-balance.

He rose from the blanket, feeling the need for some distance. She looked at him in surprise. ''What are you doing?'' she asked.

''Going for a walk. I think better when I walk. I'll be back in a little while.'' He headed out toward a jogging path, wondering why in the world the woman he'd come to divorce still managed to fill him with such depths of emotion.

Claire blew out a sigh of frustration and sat back on her haunches. She was on her knees on the floor of the basement of City Hall, surrounded by box after box of old documents, newspapers and miscellany from the past.

Bertha Bellew had been a one-woman historical society and had made an attempt at organizing the material, but unfortunately Bertha had passed away several years ago. Since that time, the old records and documents had been shuffled and reboxed and rearranged without much regard.

She'd already gone through two boxes of items and had found nothing from the year 1856. At this rate it would take her months to find out anything about Sarah and Daniel Walker and she certainly didn't want Joshua hanging around for months. It was bad enough that he'd already been in the house for almost a week.

Six days, to be exact. Joshua had been in the house for six days and never had Claire's nerves been stretched so taut. His presence seemed to have taken over every corner of the house. His scent seemed to have permeated the nooks and crevices of the very structure itself.

There were times when they were all together in the evenings, that she almost felt as if it were five years ago and Joshua had never left her. And that irritated her more than anything.

She pulled herself up from the floor, deciding it was time to pack it in for the day. It was almost dinnertime and even though Joshua had insisted that he would be in charge of the evening meal, she couldn't remember a time he'd ever cooked anything substantial in the past.

Tomorrow morning the new clue for the treasure hunt would appear in the morning paper. She wanted to get a good night's sleep so she could get up bright and early to read the latest clue.

As she walked home, the sun bore down on her with an unusually intense heat, portending the mid-summer days to come. She faced the summer with dread. So far she and Sarge had managed to get through the days without the air-conditioning, but it wouldn't be long before they would need to turn it on and that meant higher electric bills.

She thought of all the checks Joshua had sent her over the years. Whenever she'd received one, she'd instantly ripped it into tiny shreds and placed it in her 'confetti box,' an empty tissue box that held the tiny tatters of both checks and letters he'd sent to her.

She'd thought the checks were guilt money from him and that somehow in cashing them, she would be helping him assuage his guilt over leaving her.

Maybe she'd been selfish in not cashing them

and using the money to make things easier for Sarge, but hurt and bitterness had tainted any decisions she had made where Joshua McCane had been concerned. Now, with a droplet of sweat scooting down her back beneath her cotton T-shirt, she wished she hadn't been so stubborn where that money had been concerned.

I just need to find that treasure, she told herself. That money, although certainly not a fortune, would make everything okay.

As she entered the house, the first sound she heard was laughter coming from the kitchen. She paused on the threshold of the front door, for a moment savoring the sound that had been almost nonexistent in the house for the past five years.

Joshua had always been good at evoking laughter. Even though he had the good looks of a matinee idol, he had the heart and soul of a witty comedian.

She leaned against the door, for a moment remembering when he'd entertain her with fanciful stories of make-believe creatures and crazy worlds.

She hated to admit it, but she'd missed his stories and his laughter. And if she looked deep within her heart, she'd find that she'd missed him, too. But that didn't mean she ever intended to invite him back into her heart or her life again.

Steeling herself for the onslaught of seeing him again, she squared her shoulders and walked into the kitchen. For the first time since walking through the front door she became aware of the odor of fresh garlic, minced onion and spicy tomato sauce.

Joshua stood at the stove and Sarge was at the table as she walked into the kitchen. "Something smells marvelous."

Joshua smiled and moved a large pot off the stove burner. "My world-famous tomato sauce."

"I didn't know you had a world-famous tomato sauce," she said as she sank down at the table.

"This is my first time trying it out," he replied.

"We're guinea pigs, Cookie," Sarge exclaimed with more spirit than he'd shown in months. "We're either going to have a great meal or we'll all be sick with ptomaine poisoning."

Joshua laughed. "I don't think I'm in danger of poisoning anyone, but as much garlic as I used we won't have to worry about vampires."

His light tone set the mood for the meal, which consisted of spaghetti, salad and garlic bread. As they ate, Joshua told them about the latest game he was working on, an educational one based on opposites.

Despite her desire to remain immune from his charm, she found herself studying him as he talked about his work, noting how his features became animated with excitement. She found herself laughing as he spoke of some of his most popular games, with creatures apparently as colorful as their silly names.

"No blood or guts in DreamQuest games," he explained. "And good always triumphs over evil and love always wins the day."

Maybe in his games, she thought. But not in real life. Sometimes love died, or wasn't as strong as one thought, or couldn't survive beneath the weight of life and loss and grief.

She was grateful when Sarge indicated he was ready for bed early, as she was exhausted and more than ready not only to call it a day, but to escape Joshua's company.

She got Sarge into bed for the night, then went into her own room. The same room where she and Joshua had once slept and made love and spun dreams and fantasies of their future.

The room was overly warm, with no breeze stirring the curtains at the window. Despite the warmth, she fell asleep almost immediately.

She awoke with a start, unsure what had awakened her, but filled with a yearning that pierced her soul. Surely it's the heat, she thought as she sat up and lifted her heavy hair from the nape of her neck.

It was just after midnight, but she instinctively knew that sleep would not return easily. She got out of bed and pulled on a lightweight cotton robe.

As she opened her bedroom door, the house greeted her with quiet darkness. While he'd been here, Joshua had been a late-nighter and she was grateful he had apparently gone to bed.

Without turning on any lights, unwilling to alert anyone that she was awake, she padded into the kitchen and poured herself a glass of orange juice from the fridge, then carried it out to the front porch.

As she sank down on the top step of the porch, she was grateful to feel a cool breeze that stirred her hair and caressed her face. She closed her eyes and raised her head, allowing the breeze to flow over her neck, and she suddenly remembered the dream she'd had just before awakening.

It had once again been about them—about Sarah and Daniel. She opened her eyes and took a sip of her juice, irritated that the couple not only invaded her thoughts during the day, but filled her dreams at night, as well.

It was almost as if she had some sort of strange, cosmic connection with them, a connection she didn't understand. How was it possible that there would be any connection between herself and an old photograph?

"Can't sleep?" Joshua's deep voice came from the doorway. Before she could reply, he opened the door and eased down beside her on the stoop.

He was bare-chested and wearing only a pair of shorts. He smelled of shampoo, fresh-scented soap and a touch of spicy cologne.

"I think maybe the heat woke me," she replied and set her juice glass between them, as if to serve as a barrier. "What about you?"

"I hadn't really tried sleeping yet. I was just about to get into bed when I thought I heard somebody creeping around." He stretched his legs out before him. "It's beautiful out here tonight."

She nodded absently, her thoughts still consumed with the lingering memories of her dream. "They were very young when they married—like us." She didn't realize she'd spoken aloud until she saw the confusion on Joshua's face. "Daniel and Sarah Walker. I've been dreaming about them a lot."

"Really? What kind of dreams?" He moved her juice glass and slid closer to her.

"I don't know, just dreams about them." She didn't want to tell him that what she dreamed about was the love they shared for each other, a love that was so strong, so passionate that it transcended time and place.

It was the kind of love she'd once thought she and Joshua shared, but she'd been wrong.

"How do you know they married young?" His green eyes glowed in the moonlight as he gazed at her.

Her heart still filled with the sweet longings that her dream had evoked, she was far too conscious of his nearness. "I saw it in my dream," she replied softly. "I saw their wedding. I've been dreaming about them ever since we found their picture." She forced a small burst of laughter. "Crazy, huh? I'm sure it's just an overactive imagination at work."

"An overactive imagination, that's always been my department," he observed with a smile.

The smile was as warm as the night and she knew she should escape, go back into her room and fall back into dreams that had no capacity to hurt her.

But she didn't leave and for long moments they sat side by side in a strangely companionable silence. "What happened to the porch swing?" he asked, finally breaking the quiet.

"It's in the garage. It was getting pretty old and rickety." It was a half-truth and she didn't look at him as she said it. The full truth was that she'd taken down the swing soon after Joshua had left, unable to face the place where she and Joshua had spent many a night, enjoying the seasons that had passed, the season of their love.

"Have you dated, Claire, in the time I've been away?"

She looked at him sharply. "Of course not. Aside from the fact that I have no desire to date, we *are* still married."

His gaze studied her intently. "Why haven't you asked me for a divorce?"

She shrugged and stared out into the darkness of the night. "Because it doesn't matter to me whether we're divorced or not. I don't plan on ever dating or getting remarried."

"You're way too young to make a decision not to marry again," he replied.

She didn't counter him, although she knew her decision was right, and she would never change her mind about not marrying again. "What about you? Have you been dating one of those half-naked California girls?"

"Of course not. I'm still a married man." His gaze held hers intently and in the depths of his beautiful green eyes she saw a spark of heat.

She had instinctively known he wouldn't have dated. Joshua was a man of honor and had often told her how deeply he'd believed in the sanctity of marriage.

He reached out and caressed a strand of her hair and her mouth went achingly dry. The soft, familiar stroke of his hand created a quivering inside her. "We're still married, Claire," he murmured.

She knew he was going to kiss her, read it in his eyes as he leaned toward her. She had only a split second to jump up and run, but she was frozen in place. She was unable to deny the tiny part of her that wanted his kiss just one last time.

Before she could fully accept the fact that she

wanted this to happen, his lips were on hers, plying hers with the hot, sweet taste of desire.

Instantly, her heart ached with the sweet familiarity of kissing Joshua. Her breasts tingled and every nerve ending in her entire body became electrified, as if in anticipation of making love.

When his arms reached to enfold her, she managed to break the inertia that had momentarily gripped her. She jumped up and took an unsteady step away from him.

"You shouldn't have done that, Joshua," she said, appalled to hear her voice slightly breathless.

He stood, but didn't attempt to breach the distance that separated them. "Why not? I've wanted to do it since the moment I saw you again. And if I'm not mistaken, a minute ago you were not only not protesting, but you were kissing me back."

A blush warmed her cheeks. "You caught me off-guard. I didn't have a chance to protest."

It was a lie and she knew it. She'd had a moment when she could have circumvented his kiss, but she hadn't.

She knew by the look on his face he didn't believe her and a surge of defensive anger rose up inside her. "We might still be married, Joshua, but that doesn't mean we have a marriage. And as far as I'm concerned, we'll never have a marriage again."

She didn't wait for his reply, but instead turned

and ran away from him, into the house. Retreating into the safe privacy of her bedroom, she tore off her robe and crawled back into bed.

The taste of his mouth still lingered on her own and she fought the childish impulse to scrub at her mouth with the back of her hand. That action wouldn't erase the sweet sensations of his kiss, nor would it dispel the knowledge that for just a moment, she'd wanted his arms around her. For just the time between heartbeats she'd wished they could go back in time and be young and happy and in love once again.

# Chapter Five

"'Like a witch's mane that blows in the air. Dig at the base and the treasure is there.'" Joshua read aloud the latest clue in the morning paper.

The three of them were seated at the kitchen table. Sarge was enjoying his usual bowl of oatmeal, as Claire and Joshua were having coffee.

"'Witch's mane...'" Claire repeated thoughtfully. "Anything about witches always makes me think of Hazel Benton."

"Crazier than a loon, that woman was," Sarge quipped. "I've met a lot of queer women in my time, but old Hazel was the queen of the weird."

"All I know is that she had every kid in town scared spitless of her," Joshua said.

"She had most of the adults in town scared spitless of her, too," Sarge replied. "She thought she had special powers, thought she could read people's minds and communicate with spirits. More than once I had to have a little talk with her about assault."

"Assault? Why, what would she do?" Claire asked. She looked lovely, clad in a pair of white shorts and a turquoise blouse that turned her eyes more blue than their usual smoke-gray.

"She'd be shopping in town and pass some poor hapless man and whack him on the back or slap him in the face because she'd supposedly read his mind, and he was entertaining lustful thoughts about her." Sarge laughed and shook his head ruefully. "She was some piece of work. Used to fly a flag at half-staff all the time, said she was mourning the troubled undead who hadn't crossed over to the other side."

"A flag?" Joshua frowned. "I don't remember her having a flag."

"She took the flagpole down years ago when she decided it was a conductor for alien energy or some such nonsense."

"'Like a witch's mane that blows in the air'…like a flag?" Joshua looked at Claire.

"And the clue about ashes, Hazel's house is now in ashes." She sat up straighter in her chair, her eyes sparkling with excitement. "Do you think the treasure is there?"

"Sarge, do you remember where the flagpole stood on Hazel's property?" Joshua asked.

"Sure, it was just off her patio in a flower bed in the backyard."

Joshua looked at Claire once again. "I'd say that's the place we should look next."

Claire shot a glance at Sarge. "I'll just wait here and you can go see if it's there."

"Nonsense, we're in this treasure hunt together, Cookie. I saw Mrs. Iverson getting her paper when I picked up yours, so I know she's up and dressed. I'm sure she wouldn't mind coming over here for a half hour or forty-five minutes while we check out Hazel's backyard."

"You're going to stick me with that creature again?" Sarge asked, although there was no venom in his voice at all.

"Sarge, that's not nice," Claire said.

"The woman treats me like a damned invalid."

"Maybe that's because you're in that wheel-chair," Joshua observed. "If you'd get some physical therapy and get out of that chair, she wouldn't treat you like an invalid."

Sarge frowned thoughtfully. "Then I suppose you should set up an appointment for physical therapy for me, Cookie."

Claire looked at Joshua, obviously surprised by the old man's capitulation. "I'll call the hospital and set it up right now."

"And while she's doing that, I'll go next door

and see if Mrs. Iverson can come over for a little while.'' Joshua got up from the table and headed out the back door.

Twenty minutes later he and Claire set off down the sidewalk. Although it was just after eight, the sun was already warm on his shoulders. He had a garden trowel tucked in the back pocket of his jean shorts and hoped if the treasure was around the base of the flagpole at Hazel's that it wasn't buried too deep.

''I'm not sure how you got Sarge to agree to start going to physical therapy, but I'm grateful that he's finally agreed to go,'' Claire said. ''I've been trying to get him into therapy at the hospital since his stroke.''

Joshua smiled. ''Ah, but you were probably using logic and reason to try to get him to go. I merely appealed to his male vanity. I think he has a crush on Mrs. Iverson.''

''No way,'' Claire replied with a disbelieving burst of laughter. ''You heard what he calls her.''

''Yeah, but I thought I detected a bit of affection in his voice.''

A tiny thoughtful frown creased her forehead. ''Now that you mention it, Wilma is always doing little things for Sarge. Although she constantly tells him he's a crabby old coot.''

''Her husband passed away before I left Mayfield. She's been alone a long time. Maybe there's a bit of romance blooming.''

For a few minutes they walked in silence down the shade-dappled walk toward Hazel's property. Joshua found himself thinking about the kiss they'd shared the night before. It had been everything he remembered...and more.

Someplace in the back of his mind, he'd thought that kissing her again would somehow release him from his memories of the past—finally and forever release him from her. But there had been no release. Rather, the kiss had merely served to deepen his ambivalence where she was concerned.

He wanted her, but after five years of abstinence, was that really so strange? Anyway, even after all this time, the thought of making love to anyone other than Claire seemed alien and somehow wrong.

He couldn't quite imagine what life would be like if he tried to get back with her, nor could he quite imagine what his future would be like without her in it.

"You've gotten very quiet," she said, breaking into his thoughts.

"Just thinking," he said.

He wondered what would happen if he said his name? In the days that he'd been back in Mayfield staying with Claire, neither of them had spoken his name once.

He gazed at her, as always enjoying the play of sunshine in her beautiful hair. "Do you think about him, Claire?" he asked softly.

Her footsteps faltered just enough for him to know she knew exactly who he meant. He held his breath, unsure if he should expect some sort of an explosion.

There was a long moment of silence, then she expelled a tiny sigh. "I think of Sammy every day," she finally replied. The name hung in the air, bringing with it memories of both incredible joy and indescribable pain.

"I wake up in the morning," she continued, "and in that instant before full awakeness grips me, I find myself listening for him."

Joshua reached out and took her hand in his. For a second he thought she was going to pull her hand away. Instead her fingers entwined with his, but she kept her gaze averted from him.

"I remember how first thing in the morning he'd stand up in his crib and yell 'Dada.'"

"Mama," she countered, a ghost of a smile curving her lips. "He'd shout 'Mama.'"

It was an ancient argument, a bantering from the past that had always been delivered good-naturedly. Nearly every morning for the two years of Sammy's life, Joshua and Claire had each tried to take possession of Sammy's words.

"You remember the morning he fell out of bed?" She looked at him, her eyes shining.

How well Joshua remembered that morning. He and Claire had been indulging in a bout of pre-dawn lovemaking when they'd heard a thud. Horrified, the two of them had raced from their bedroom into Sammy's, terrified of what they might find.

"I'll never forget that little face smiling at us from beneath the crib," Joshua said. Sammy had been under the crib, clutching Mr. Peaches, his favorite stuffed animal and laughing that he 'go boom.'

Claire stopped walking and faced him, her features a mix of both bittersweet joy and a whisper of sadness. "We made a beautiful baby, didn't we, Joshua?"

"We did, Cookie." He reached for her and she went willingly into his arms. He smelled the sweet sunshine in her hair, felt the warmth of her body and realized this was the first time since they'd buried their son that he'd held her in his arms.

They stood there on the sidewalk for long moments, wrapped in an embrace that felt as medicinal, as healing as a hot poultice on a congested chest.

She pulled away first, stepping back from him, an irritated frown creasing the center of her forehead. "We need to get to Hazel's and see if the treasure is there. I don't like leaving Sarge for too long." There was a steely strength in her eyes, the same strength that had attracted him to her when they'd been young. It was also the same strength that had eventually driven him away.

*    *    *

As they finished the walk to Hazel's place in silence, Claire tried to forget how it had felt once again to be held in Joshua's arms. His body against hers had been so achingly familiar, and, for just a moment, as his arms had enfolded her close, she'd felt safe and loved.

Illusion, she reminded herself. It had been memories of Sammy that had made them seek each other's embrace. She wasn't sure what Joshua was doing—holding her and kissing her—but she knew it had nothing to do with love.

If he'd loved her, he never would have walked away from her five years ago. If he'd really loved her, he never would have stayed away for so long.

She knew the truth in her heart. He'd married her because she was pregnant. While he'd been a good husband and father while Sammy was alive, once Sammy was gone there had been nothing to keep him with her.

She could not allow herself to become vulnerable to Joshua. Besides, the decisions she'd made for herself concerning her own future had left no place for a man. She tamped down her thoughts and focused on the surroundings.

There was very little left of Hazel's house. What had been a grand two-story Victorian home was now nothing more than a pile of rubble. The only thing left standing was a stone chimney that rose high in the air.

''Why hasn't the city removed this mess?''

Joshua asked as they walked around the skeleton left by the fire.

"Who knows? I've heard that Hazel refuses to allow anything to be done because she believes that fire spirits are now living here. I've also heard that Mayfield doesn't have the money in its coffers to take legal action to get something done."

"Sarge said the old flagpole was in the backyard by the patio," Joshua said, motioning her to follow him around the side of the house.

Despite the weeds that scratched her bare legs, a new sense of excitement rose up inside Claire as she thought of the possibility of digging up the money.

Maybe with a little of the money she could start to take a few classes and begin working toward a teaching degree. She'd always wanted to teach history. She and Joshua had agreed that when Sammy was old enough for preschool, Claire would get the college education she desired. But, of course, fate had intervened.

The backyard was hopelessly overgrown and bordered on three sides by ancient woods. "I think maybe I should have packed a machete along with your trusty trowel," Joshua exclaimed.

Claire frowned, slightly dismayed as she gazed at the landscape. "I can't imagine Clark Windsloe crawling around in these weeds to bury anything back here."

"Ah, but maybe that's exactly what he wants

everyone to think,'' Joshua countered. ''A treasure hunt that's too easy isn't fun at all. I've learned that with my games. If an adventure is too hard, kids quit trying. If it's too easy, then it's just no fun.''

''I'm glad you're doing so well,'' Claire said and it was true. Until his alcoholic uncle had moved away and left Joshua on his own, he had suffered through a miserable childhood. He deserved to have good things happening to him now.

''I owe a lot of it to you,'' he replied.

''How do you figure?'' They'd reached the patio, a ten-by-twelve flooring of large red bricks.

He pulled the trowel from his back pocket, his gaze lingering on hers. ''You always liked to listen to my silly stories and encouraged me to tell you more.''

''I thought you might eventually become a children's book author.''

''I might have if I hadn't taken that computer class and discovered the fun of creating games.'' He directed his gaze to the area around the patio. ''Now let's see if we can't find you that treasure.''

It took them twenty minutes of searching to finally find the old base of the flagpole. Claire eyed it in dismay. ''There's no way somebody buried anything here recently,'' she said, fighting against a wave of disappointment.

''It's been a month since the first clue appeared in the paper. Grass and weeds can get pretty overgrown in a month's time.'' Joshua knelt down and began to dig around the base, but she knew his efforts were useless.

Still, she watched silently, reluctantly enjoying the way the muscles in his back and arms grew taut each time he drove the trowel into the hard earth.

Realizing she was enjoying the sight of him far too much, she averted her gaze and instead stared off toward the woods at the back of the yard.

A slight breeze whispered in her ear and she tilted her head as she thought she heard the murmur of voices. Her body warmed with a sudden wave of heat, an electric charge like that she felt each time she held Sarah and Daniel's picture in her fingers.

She closed her eyes for a moment, and when she opened them again, the trees before her were smaller, less dense, and there was a clearing in the middle, a clearing where a crowd of people were gathered. There was a large table laden with food and laughter rode the air.

Somewhere in the back of her mind, she knew it wasn't real, but the sound of the laughter, the mouthwatering scents of the food seemed as concrete as the clothes on her body.

Then she saw them...herself and Joshua...no, Sarah and Daniel. They stood near the table in a group of other people. Sarah was clad in a long blue gingham dress and held in her arms a baby with curly blond ringlets. Daniel stood next to her, his face a study of proud fatherhood, of sweet love.

As Daniel gazed at Sarah, Claire felt his love filling her up and the sweetest emotion rushed through her. I'll love you forever. Although she couldn't hear the words from Daniel, she felt them in her heart, in her soul.

"Claire!" A warm, strong hand grabbed her forearm.

She blinked, and the vision before her vanished. Joshua stood before her, a worry line creasing his forehead. "Are you all right?" he asked, his hand still warm on her arm.

"I'm fine," she replied, her voice sounding faint and faraway to her own ears.

"Are you sure? You looked as if you were in a trance or something." He removed his hand from her, his gaze still worried.

"I'm okay," she said, although she didn't feel okay. She felt rather lightheaded and wondered what on earth had caused her to see what wasn't there, why she was seeing visions of Sarah and Daniel's life. "Really…I'm fine." She forced a reassuring smile to her lips.

He eyed her for another long minute, then gestured toward the flagpole base, where it was obvious he'd been digging for some time, making her wonder how long she'd been lost in the vision. "I dug all around the base, but there's nothing there."

She nodded and looked at him once again, noting that his T-shirt was damp with sweat from his exertions. "You look hot. Let's get back and I'll make a big pitcher of iced tea."

"When we get back to the house, I'm cranking up the air conditioner." He held up the trowel to still her automatic protest. "I'll pay the utility bill and you aren't going to argue with me about it. I hate this heat and it can't be good for Sarge, either."

She wanted to protest, but he'd used ammunition she couldn't deny. He was right, the heat couldn't be good for Sarge, and for Sarge she would accept his offer. "Thank you," she replied stiffly. "But when I find the treasure money, I'll pay you back."

"You don't have to repay me. Don't worry, Claire, I understand you don't want to accept anything from me, but I'll do whatever it takes to make Sarge comfortable, pay whatever it takes to get him back on his feet."

With each word he spoke his eyes grew darker and Claire felt smaller. "I'm sorry," she said. "I didn't mean to make you angry."

He swiped a hand through his hair and drew a deep breath. "I've just always found your self-sufficiency rather irritating."

"Let's not start on what we found irritating about each other," she replied with a smile, hoping to break the tension that had sprung up between them. She didn't want to fight with him. In fact, she wasn't sure exactly what she wanted from him.

Nothing, she told herself as they left Hazel's and started walking back to the house. She didn't want anything from Joshua McCane. And yet, even while she told herself that, she couldn't deny that for a moment, as he'd held her in his arms, she hadn't wanted him to stop.

The self-sufficiency he'd said irritated him was the coping mechanism that had gotten her through her early life. As they headed back to the house in silence, her thoughts drifted back to when she'd been eight years old and her parents had been killed in a car accident.

At that early age, she'd learned never to depend on anyone, never to need anyone. She loved Sarge and she had once loved Joshua, but she'd made a vow to herself long ago that she would never, ever need anyone.

"I thought maybe I'd spend a little time at City Hall this afternoon if you don't mind staying with Sarge for a while." More than anything she felt the desire to get some sort of information about Sarah and Daniel Walker. She wanted to know what it was about them that had her dreaming about them, seeing visions about them. She wanted to know why they looked like her and Joshua, why they seemed to be haunting her.

Besides, once she got that information, perhaps Joshua would leave, go back to California. She didn't even care any longer if he helped her find the treasure.

"That's fine," he agreed.

She cast him a sideways glance, a slight breathlessness sweeping over her as she took in his utter attractiveness. She'd felt that same crazy breathlessness the very first time she'd seen him. And when the corners of his lips had curled up in a smile directed at her, she'd thought she might die.

"Surely you have to get back to California soon," she said. "I mean, how can you run a successful business based there from here?"

He flashed his green gaze in her direction, a small smile of amusement dancing on his lips. "There's no hurry. Not only do I have terrific people working for me, but with modern technology and my laptop, I'm in touch with people at DreamQuest every day."

"But communicating through e-mail and actually being there are two different things," she replied.

"Actually, I've been thinking about opening a branch office of the business here in Mayfield."

She stumbled in her tracks and looked at him in surprise. "You're kidding?" Did that mean he would remain full-time in Mayfield? It had been difficult enough seeing him and spending time with him over the past week. How would she ever survive seeing him every day for the rest of her life?

"I haven't made up my mind yet, but it's something I'm kicking around in my head. Mayfield could certainly use the revenue that a new business would bring in.''

While that was certainly true, Claire didn't even want to contemplate Joshua living here full-time. While she was certain the two of them could have no future together, she couldn't imagine being a witness to him dating, falling in love, marrying and beginning a family with another woman. And there was no doubt in her mind that eventually that would happen.

From the moment she and Joshua had begun to date, she had known how important family was to him, since he had grown up with none of his own. When he'd started seeing Claire he'd quickly adopted Sarge, then planned a life with at least four children with her. In fact, they had been planning for their second child when Sammy had passed away.

''I would think that Mayfield was a little too small-town for you after your years on the West Coast,'' she said as they turned onto the walk that led up to their house.

''I've always been a small-town boy at heart, and so many of the happiest memories of my life are here.'' They stopped on the porch and for a moment she thought he was going to reach for her again, pull her against his big, strong chest.

''You can't live with just your memories,'' she said softly, appalled to realize she half wished he *would* reach out for her. ''Memories are nothing more than ashes of the past, and the past is dead and gone forever.''

''You can't really believe that,'' he replied softly. He reached out and stroked his fingers through the strands of her hair, his hand coming precariously close to her breast. ''What about the idea of reincarnation, or the fact that the past can sometimes be a pathway to the future?''

His eyes radiated a softness that frightened her because for just a moment she wanted to fall into that softness, fall into the sweet memories that resided there.

*I'll love you forever.* The words ached in her heart, but she knew they weren't Joshua's words to her. They were Daniel's words for Sarah, words from a vision that had nothing to do with her and Joshua.

She stepped away from him, her pulse racing from his touch. ''That sounds like a bunch of crazy New Age nonsense to me,'' she replied, then frowned thoughtfully.

''On second thought, maybe you're right. But if the past is a pathway to the future, then it would be wise to understand the mistakes you made in the past and never repeat them again.'' A hard knot formed in her chest as she continued. ''We were a mistake, Joshua. You were a mistake I have no intention of repeating.''

She opened the front door and went inside, leaving him standing on the front porch alone.

# Chapter Six

Joshua wondered what in the heck he was doing as he hung the new porch swing he'd ordered and had delivered from the lumberyard.

Claire was at City Hall researching Sarah and Daniel Walker and Sarge was in his bedroom napping. The first thing Joshua'd done when they'd gotten back from Hazel's place was crank up the air conditioner in the house, and the rooms were now comfortably cool.

So, what was he doing out in the midday heat hanging a swing she probably wouldn't want? Why was he even contemplating remaining when she'd made it crystal-clear she didn't want him here?

The answer that sprang into his mind, that he

was still in love with her, perhaps would always be in love with her, certainly didn't make him happy.

He finished hanging the swing, then sat down, trying to figure out exactly why he was still here in Mayfield, here with Claire.

The answer came like a thunderclap in his head. He hadn't come back to Mayfield to tell her he wanted a divorce. He'd come back for a reconciliation. He'd come back because he loved her and he wanted to build a life with her once again.

In the years that he'd been away, not a day had passed that she hadn't been in his thoughts. For months after he'd walked away from her, he'd imagined the scent of her on his skin. For months after he'd left, he'd wake up in the morning and reach for her, only to be met with the cold reality of empty arms in an empty bed.

In the week that he'd been here she'd told him in a thousand different ways that she didn't want him back, and yet here he remained.

It had been the kiss. Perhaps he might have already packed his bags and returned to California if they hadn't kissed. She might be telling him she couldn't wait for him to leave, but when her lips had been against his, she'd spoken something far different.

And that's why he was still here, because he wasn't sure she was ready to tell him goodbye forever, either. But he wasn't a foolish man. He knew he couldn't make things work between them if she didn't want them to work. No matter how much he wanted her, he couldn't force her to want him back. That painful realization was what had finally made him leave almost three months after Sammy's death.

A noise behind him snagged his attention and he turned in the swing to see Wilma Iverson approaching, a pie tin in her hands.

He stood and smiled a greeting. "Ah, it looks like you come bearing gifts," he said.

"For Sarge. I know he's partial to apple pie." She climbed the porch stairs and eyed the new swing with approval. "There's nothing better than sitting on a porch swing on a starry night, is there?"

"As far as I'm concerned, it's the next best thing to heaven," he replied, then gestured to the pie she held. "Is Sarge allowed to eat that?"

She sniffed indignantly. "I wouldn't bring over something he wasn't allowed to eat. It's sugarless and he can eat it in moderation." She headed for the door. "Is he awake?"

Joshua shook his head. "He's napping."

"Sit down. I'll just set it on the table in the kitchen." She disappeared inside, then returned a moment later and to his surprise, eased down next to him on the swing.

She smelled like cinnamon and vanilla, a pleasant combination that instantly made his mouth water for a piece of her freshly baked pie.

"Where's Claire? I saw her take off from here earlier."

"She's down at City Hall, going through some of the old records they have in the basement. We found an old photo of a couple and she's trying to learn what she can about them."

"She always did like history stuff." Wilma shook her head and shoved her feet against the porch to set the swing swaying with an energetic rhythm that nearly set him flying off. "It's not right," she exclaimed.

"What's not right?" Joshua asked as he grabbed the chain to balance himself on the swiftly swinging seat.

"It's not right that a young woman like Claire is cooped up inside all the time with her ailing grandfather. But you can't tell her anything. Like peas in a pod, her and Sarge are both pigheaded and independent to a fault."

"Amen," Joshua replied.

She halted the swing by planting her feet firmly on the porch. Had they been in a car they would have skidded to a halt and Joshua would have shot through the front windshield. As it was, he nearly left the swing, not of his own volition.

"So, what are you going to do about it?" Her sharp blue eyes gazed at him expectantly.

He sat back, for a moment speechless. "I'm not

sure what I *can* do about it,'' he finally replied. ''As you said, they are both stubborn and independent.''

''You need to get her out of the house more. You need to make her laugh again. She's only twenty-five years old, but she's been living like an eighty-year-old woman.'' Wilma stood and headed for the stairs.

She paused and turned back to him. ''What she really needs is a man who can remind her that she's a healthy, desirable woman. My goodness, boy, you're still married to her. I've never seen a young woman who needs to be loved more than she does and you should be making love to her every night.'' With these astonishing words, she turned and headed back home.

Joshua watched her until she disappeared back into her house, stunned by the entire conversation. He was still seated on the swing twenty minutes later when he spied Claire coming down the sidewalk toward home.

All thoughts fled from his mind as he lost himself in the simple enjoyment of watching her. There was a spring to her steps that set her hips swaying, and she was clutching a piece of paper to her chest. Her hair shone like spun silk, glistening as the afternoon sun danced among the strands.

She looked like a fairy princess from one of his games. With sudden clarity he realized she *was* the princess in all of his games. Every princess, queen or good fairy in every game he'd created had been patterned after Claire.

The moment the fairy princess saw him seated on the swing, she transformed into a wicked witch. He saw the frown that took possession of her features, saw the rigid set of her shoulders as she turned onto the property.

"I see you've been busy while I've been gone," she said as she climbed the stairs to the porch.

"Lighten up, Cookie, it's just a porch swing," he replied, then patted the space next to him. "Looks like you found something. Why don't you have a seat and tell me what you've found."

He saw a battle take place inside her, knew that for some reason the porch swing had not made her happy, and she didn't seem to want to share the space with him. But on the other hand, she appeared to be excited and eager to share whatever it was she'd found in the dusty basement of City Hall.

Her excitement over what she'd found apparently won and she sat next to him, their thighs touching in the small confines.

"Wilma brought over a sugarless apple pie for Sarge," he said.

"That was nice of her."

"Yeah. She's worried about you."

She eyed him in surprise. "Worried about me? Why?"

"She thinks you don't get out enough, that you

spend too much time cooped up inside with Sarge. She thinks you've forgotten that you're a beautiful, desirable young woman.''

Her cheeks pinked and she averted her gaze from his. "She didn't say that."

"Okay, maybe I embellished a little," he said teasingly. "But she is worried about you."

"Whatever." She looked at him once again. "Want to know what I learned today about our mystery couple?"

"Sure."

For a moment she said nothing. She stared straight ahead, as if lost in thought. "I'm going to tell you something that will probably make you think I've lost my mind," she finally began.

"I'm not sure that's possible," he replied. "You've always been one of the most grounded people I know."

Again her gaze sought his and she smiled. "You may change your mind once I tell you this."

He stopped the movement of the swing, intrigued by her words. "What?"

"Ever since we found that photo of Daniel and Sarah, I've felt a strange connection to her. It's more than just the fact that she looks like me, it's something deeper…more profound. When I dream about her, it's like I feel her inside of me." She flipped a long strand of her hair behind her shoulder and looked at him, her eyes the gray of troubled skies. "It's bad enough that they invade my dreams, but this morning when we were in Hazel's backyard I was wide awake when I had a vision.''

That explained why she hadn't answered him when he'd called her several times, and the blank look that had been on her face for a worrisome few minutes when he'd finished digging around the flagpole.

"A vision?" he prompted.

She nodded. "I know it sounds completely crazy, but I saw the woods at the back of Hazel's yard and suddenly the trees were small and sparse, and there was a clearing and people were in the clearing.''

Her words tumbled over themselves, faster and faster as she explained what had happened. ''Daniel and Sarah were there along with a lot of other people, and there was a long table with food. Kids were playing tag and everyone was happy and laughing.''

She paused to take a deep breath and closed her eyes. "It was a wonderful day, a gathering of neighbors and friends to celebrate the end of a harsh winter and the welcome advent of spring.''

Her voice had taken on a peculiar singsong rhythm and the hairs on Joshua's arms raised as a strange electricity seemed to snap and crackle in the air.

"Annie Watts has brought cornbread. Daniel loves her cornbread, and Margaret and Robert

Green have brought a basket of apples that are as sweet and juicy as any I've ever tasted.''

Joshua watched her face. Her eyes were still closed and it was obvious she was in another place, another time. He wondered if he should touch her, shake her arm to pull her back to his world, but she seemed to be in no physical distress. Rather, a soft smile curved her lips as she continued.

"We have made a home here, my beloved Daniel and I, among these people in this new land. And now that we have our son, Caleb, I feel as if our life is complete.''

Joshua heard the love in her voice, but knew it was Sarah's love for Daniel that emanated from her. He'd believed she'd once felt that same depth of love for him, but time and distance had made him wonder if it had all only been an illusion, the deep desire of a lonely young man.

Her eyes flew open and she blinked once, twice, then gasped and reached for his hand. "What's happening, Joshua? Why am I seeing visions of their life?''

"I don't know," he replied softly, enjoying far too much the feel of her dainty hand in his. "Is it possible you're just imagining what their life might have been like?" he asked, seeking a rational explanation. "When I'm working on my games, sometimes it's hard for me to separate fantasy from real life.''

She shook her head vehemently. "This isn't me

imagining their life, it's me somehow experiencing their life. When I saw the vision this morning at Hazel's, I saw Sarah holding a child, a golden-haired little boy and it wasn't me imagining it. It was real! As real as you and I sitting here, and I have proof.''

She pulled her hand from his and handed him one of the papers she'd brought home with her from her search. It appeared to be part of a birth record of sorts, although the lettering was so faded it was just barely legible. There were several lines of names, but half of the document was missing.

"Here…" She pointed to a line of the fine, spidery writing. "Caleb Walker, born to Daniel and Sarah Walker on May 5, 1857. The celebration I saw in the clearing this morning must have taken place in the spring of 1858 because Caleb looked like he was about a year old.''

"What happened to the rest of the document? It looks like some of it is missing.''

"It is. I only found half of it. I'm hoping I'll find the other half eventually. So far, this is the only proof I've found that Sarah and Daniel really lived around here, but I'm sure if I spend enough time with those boxes in the basement of City Hall, I'll find out more about them.''

She took the piece of paper from him and stared at it for a long moment, then returned her gaze to him. "I just don't understand any of this,'' she said softly. "I don't understand why these people feel so important to me."

"Are you sure they aren't related somehow?" he asked.

"Yes, I'm positive." She carefully folded the copy of the birth certificate. "It's an odd feeling, isn't it? That a couple who lived over a hundred years ago looked exactly like us." She eyed him curiously. "Have you had any dreams or visions about them?"

"No, none." With Wilma's words still ringing in his ears and Claire's nearness filling his senses, he had to force himself to concentrate on their conversation. "Although I did notice one thing," he added. "When I first picked up the picture from the box where it had been buried, I felt sort of an electric tingle race up my arm."

She grabbed his hand once again. "I felt it, too. In fact, I feel it every time I touch the picture." A look of relief swept over her lovely features. "I thought it was just me." She jumped up from the swing.

"What are you doing?" he asked.

"I'm going to check on Sarge, then I'm going to get the photo and see if you still feel that charge when you pick it up."

She disappeared into the house and Joshua sat back in the swing to wait for her return. Again Wilma's words played in his mind. *You should be making love to her every night.* Yes, that's what he should be doing…loving her, making love to her and rebuilding the life they'd once had, the dreams they'd once shared.

He knew she had been angry and bitter when he'd left, knew she still retained some of that anger and bitterness. But he'd had to leave. He'd lost his son and he'd effectively lost his wife. He feared if he remained, he would eventually lose his mind, his heart, his soul.

Sammy's death had created in her an all-encompassing strength that he'd both admired and resented. Sammy's death had tapped into a vein of weakness in him that he'd found both overwhelming and humiliating. But that had been a long time ago and the wounds left by Sammy's death healed a little bit more each day.

He smiled as she stepped back out on the porch, the box they'd dug up in her hands. "Sarge still sleeping?" he asked.

She nodded and once again sat next to him on the swing. "Like a rock." For a moment she remained with the box on her lap, as if she were afraid to open it and look at the picture once again.

Again he felt her body heat wafting over him, her scent wrapping around him and a surge of desire for her swept through him. It wasn't just a desire to kiss her lips, caress her body and make sweet, passionate love to her. It was the desire to return to the life they'd once had. A life filled with laughter and dreams, with passion and tenderness.

He didn't just want Claire's body, her passion, he wanted to share each and every piece of her life.

He just didn't know if it was too late for him...for them.

He watched as she opened the box and withdrew the photo. She stared at it, gasped and it fluttered from her fingers to the porch.

"What's wrong?" he asked.

"It's changed."

Her face was as pale as he'd ever seen it. "What's changed?" he asked in alarm.

"The picture. It's different." She wrapped her arms around herself, her eyes huge as she stared at him.

He bent down and picked up the photo from the porch and looked at it, then frowned and looked at her once again. "What do you mean, it's changed?" He looked at the picture again and shrugged. "It looks the same to me."

She leaned toward him and gazed at the picture. "It's different," she repeated, her voice trembling slightly. "Look here," she said pointing. "Before, his hand was on the back of the chair, now it's on her shoulder. And before he was staring straight ahead at the camera. Now look! He's looking at her."

Joshua frowned, trying to remember what he'd seen in the photograph before, but all he remembered was that it had been of two people who looked like him and Claire. He wasn't sure about the exact positions they had been in or where exactly they had been looking.

Certainly, in the picture, Daniel was looking at Sarah and the expression on his face reflected what Joshua felt in his heart for Claire— Love and sweet longing.

"Joshua, I swear to you, that picture is different than it was when we first dug it up." Her eyes bored into his intently. "I studied it and they are different than they were."

Joshua stared down at the picture once again and felt the familiar strange warm current seeping up his arm. He wasn't imagining it. It was as real as his heartbeat, which quickened in response.

"I don't know what to tell you, Cookie," he said softly. "I feel an energy flowing from it."

"So, you believe me. It has changed since last time I looked at it." Her gray eyes held a silent appeal, and he knew it was important to her that he believe her.

"I do believe you." And he did.

"But how is all of this possible?"

He placed the photo back in the box and closed it, then leaned down and set it on the porch next to the swing. "I don't know, Cookie. But I'll tell you this, every day I work on games where magic is involved, in worlds where anything is possible."

He took her hands in his. "Maybe this picture is somehow magical. I mean, how else to explain the fact that a couple who lived over a hundred years ago looks exactly like us. How else to explain the energy we both feel when we touch it.'' He tightened his grip on her hands, using his thumbs to caress the backs of them.

''We used to have magic, Claire. The two of us used to be magic together.''

She winced, as if his touch hurt her, and pulled her hands away from his. Her eyes were dark, deep. ''Maybe we did once have magic, Joshua.'' Her voice was strong and sure. ''But the magic I might have had once in my life disappeared on the day that Sammy died, and any magic that might have lingered was destroyed on the day you walked out on me.''

She stepped backward, away from the swing, but still facing him. ''I don't believe in magic anymore, Joshua. No changing picture, or magic potion or unicorn will make me believe in magic again. And now I need to go inside and check on Sarge. Are you coming?''

''I'll be there in a few minutes,'' he said. As she disappeared into the house, he set the swing swaying once again, his thoughts scattered.

He had no explanation for the picture and what Claire believed was behind its transformation. Nor could he begin to explain why Sarah and Daniel Walker looked like him and Claire.

But he suddenly knew why he had been brought back here. It had been his belief in magic that had gotten him through the hell of his childhood with his drunken, abusive uncle. And if he was responsible for stealing away Claire's belief in magic, then it was his duty to do everything in his power to return that belief to her.

The only problem was, he couldn't know if he would be returning it to her so that they could find happiness together again, or if he was returning it to her so she could find happiness with some other man.

# Chapter Seven

"Still haven't found what you're looking for?"

Claire looked up from the box she'd been digging in and saw Marie Kincaid, the city clerk, standing in the basement doorway. "I'm not exactly sure what I'm looking for, but I know I haven't found it yet," she replied as she rose and dusted off her bottom. "Everything is such a mess down here."

Marie nodded. "It's a shame, isn't it? All this history just sitting down here in boxes getting all mildewed and faded. Every once in a while Clark mentions that he wouldn't mind hiring somebody to get these things scanned and logged into a computer."

"Really?" Claire looked at her with interest. "You think he's serious about hiring somebody?"

"I think he's serious whenever he thinks about it," Marie replied. "Of course, I'm sure it wouldn't be a full-time position, but if it's something you might be interested in, you should go upstairs and talk to him. He's in his office right now."

"Thanks. I'll just put this stuff away and head upstairs to chat with him." As Marie went back upstairs, Claire carefully returned the items she'd been going through.

The idea of working part-time here amid these treasures from the past pleased her. Perhaps she could arrange it so she could work during the hours while Sarge was at physical therapy. She could certainly put the little bit of extra money to good use.

When she'd left the house an hour earlier, Joshua had been loading Sarge into the car to take him to his first physical therapy session. She hoped it wouldn't take long for Sarge to get his strength back and get out of the wheelchair.

She stifled a yawn with the back of her hand. She hadn't slept much for the past two nights. Not only had she been deeply disturbed by the photograph of Sarah and Daniel, but she'd also had been haunted by dreams of Joshua.

Her dreams had been erotic, memories and fantasies of the two of them making love. She'd awakened each morning with a hunger for his kiss, a yearning for his touch, and that was definitely disturbing.

She'd meant it when she'd told him she no longer believed in magic or happy endings. She couldn't forget the devastation he'd left behind when he'd walked out on her. As far as she was concerned, there was no going back, no magic to be reclaimed.

Thirty minutes later she was on her way home and in possession of a new part-time job. She and Clark had agreed that she would work twenty hours a week for a respectable hourly wage. As long as the hours meshed with Sarge's physical therapy, she was more than willing to take the job on.

It was just after ten-thirty when she walked into the house. Joshua greeted her in the living room, a secretive smile curving his lips. "Come on into the kitchen," he said. "I've got a surprise for you."

"A surprise? Did you figure out where the treasure is buried?" she asked eagerly.

"No, it isn't anything like that." His eyes twinkled merrily. "But I think you'll be pleased."

Curious, she followed him into the kitchen where she was astonished to see a beauty-salon chair against the sink counter. "Welcome to Joshua's hair care," he said, looking immensely pleased with himself. "I believe you're my next appointment."

He gestured her to sit, but she hesitated. "Where did you get the chair?" she asked.

"Betty's shop. She was more than happy to rent it to me for a couple of hours."

"Why did you rent it?"

He took her by the shoulders and led her to the chair, then gently nudged her to sit. "Because I know how much you used to love to have somebody else wash your hair and because I also knew that you'd never allow me to pay for an appointment at the beauty shop for you."

"So, you paid to rent a chair? What makes you think I'm going to let you wash my hair?" she asked with as much indignation as she could muster.

He smiled again. "Because I see how much you'd like it shining from your eyes, and why on earth would you deny me the pleasure of washing your hair and you the pleasure of having it washed after I've gone to all this trouble?"

He knew her too well, she thought as she relented and leaned her head back. Of all the things she'd given up when Sarge had become so ill and money had become so tight, her trips to the beauty shop had been the most missed. There was nothing nicer than having somebody else wash, dry and comb your hair.

She closed her eyes as Joshua turned on the water in the sink and tried to ignore the intimate closeness. His broad chest was at eye level as he leaned over her to adjust the water temperature.

His scent, that sexy mix of clean male and expensive cologne, filled her senses as his hands gently swept her hair out from under her shoulders and into the sink.

He began to spray her hair with water that was the perfect temperature and she squeezed her eyes more tightly closed, trying to ignore how his nearness, his scent and his body heat all combined to evoke in her a stir of deep, rich desire.

As his fingers began to stroke through her hair, she found herself remembering the sweet dreams that she'd had the last two nights, dreams of Joshua's naked skin next to hers, dreams of his lips plying hers with fiery need.

"I got a job," she said in an effort to change the direction of her thoughts. She opened her eyes and looked at him. Even upside-down he looked like a hunk.

"You did? Doing what?" He squeezed the strawberry-scented shampoo she liked onto his palms, then slathered it onto her hair.

"Clark Windsloe hired me for twenty hours a week working to sort out the boxes in the basement of City Hall. I figured I could put in the hours while Sarge is at his physical therapy sessions. Clark seemed thrilled that somebody wanted to do it, and I know I'll enjoy doing it. Maybe I'll learn more about Sarah and Daniel."

"Sounds perfect." He soaped her hair from her scalp to the ends. "Like silk," he murmured, more to himself than to her. As he used his fingertips to scrub at her scalp, she closed her eyes once again and gave in to the utter bliss of relaxation that stole over her.

He had magic fingers, and she uttered a deep sigh as they seemed to find every spot on her head that might hold stress and smooth it away. She felt as if she'd been tense forever and she welcomed the release of that tension.

As long as she kept her eyes closed and wasn't looking at him, she could almost pretend she was at the beauty shop and it wasn't Joshua's sexy male body so close to hers, but rather Betty who was standing so close and washing her hair.

By the time he rinsed the suds away, she felt boneless, more relaxed than she had felt in months. He helped her to a sitting position and quickly wrapped a towel around her wet hair.

"Come on, I'll blow it dry for you," he said.

"That's not necessary," she protested half-heartedly.

"Ah, but it is. Mr. Joshua never quits until the job is done." He took her by the hand and led her out of the kitchen and down the hallway to her bedroom.

He pointed her to the bed, then went into the adjoining bathroom to get her blow dryer. As she sank down on the rose-colored bedspread, she realized this was the first time he'd been in this room since he'd returned to Mayfield.

The room had looked different when they had been together years ago. At that time the color scheme had been blue, Joshua's favorite color. Items from his pockets had been scattered across the top of the dresser, and more often than not a pair of his pants were slung across the back of the chair in the corner.

The week after he'd left, she'd packed up everything that had belonged to him. She'd bought new curtains and a bedspread, then transformed the room from *theirs* to *hers*. It was the only way she was able to sleep in the room alone.

She watched as he returned from the bathroom wielding the blow-dryer and a hairbrush. He plugged the dryer into a nearby socket, then unwound the towel from her head.

He got behind her on the bed and began to brush out the tangles in her hair. He was gentle, apparently remembering that she was tender-headed, and as he worked he was so close behind her she could feel his warm breath on the nape of her neck.

"Am I hurting you?" he asked softly, the hairbrush paused in the air.

Yes. You're hurting me with your nearness. You're making me ache inside. These thoughts whirled around inside her. "No, you aren't hurting me," she said aloud.

Once again she closed her eyes as he turned on

the blow-dryer and pointed the warm stream of air at her head. With the brush working through the strands of wet hair and the blow-dryer warming her shoulders, she once again felt a delicious languor sweep over her.

However, the languor didn't last long. As he dried her hair, he abandoned the brush and instead used his hands to rake through her hair. Time and time again, she felt the tips of his fingers on her neck, around her ears, touching her cheek. And each touch filled her with tension and heat.

He continued to stroke her hair long after she knew it was dry. She knew she should call a halt, tell him to shut off the blow-dryer and get them both off the bed and out of the bedroom, but she didn't.

When he finally shut off the blow-dryer, the silence in the room was startling. *Get up,* her brain commanded. But before she could follow through on her brain's command, he moved her hair aside and his lips pressed hotly against her neck.

"Joshua." She meant it as a protest, but instead, to her horror, it sounded like a breathless plea.

His hands caressed her shoulders as his mouth continued to roam along her neckline. "What?" he murmured, not stopping his sweet, heated kisses.

"I think the beauty session is over." Her voice trembled and her pulse raced.

"You're right. It is." Abruptly he got off the

bed and moved to stand before her. He held out a
hand to help her up, his eyes lit with an internal
flame that stirred the embers that smoldered inside
her.

She took his hand, her heart thudding wildly and
he pulled her up off the bed and against his body
in an embrace. She raised her face, thought to protest, but instantly his lips claimed hers in a deep,
soul-wrenching kiss.

Time not only stood still, but seemed to regress,
and she felt as though she were fifteen years old
again, experiencing her very first kiss with Joshua.

As it had that first time, his kiss overwhelmed
her, swept all thoughts out of her mind and filled
her with a hunger she couldn't fight.

Despite their painful past, in spite of the lingering bitterness she felt about him walking out on
her so many years ago, it took only minutes of his
lips against hers, his arms around her, for her to
get lost in him.

Joshua hadn't intended to make love to Claire
when he'd made plans to wash her hair. His sole
intention had been to do something nice for her, to
provide her some enjoyment.

But with her warm, lithe body in his arms and
her mouth opened eagerly beneath his, he had
every intention of making love to her. Stroking the
silk of her hair had stirred him to distraction, evoking memories of making love to her in the past.

When they had been married and living together, the physical side of their relationship had been intense and beautiful. She'd been his first and only lover, and he'd been her first and only.

They had grown from young, novice teenagers fumbling in the new arena of desire, to lovers experienced in the art of giving and receiving pleasure from one another.

As the memories burned hot in his mind, he pulled her closer against him, his tongue swirling with hers. The desire that had been simmering from the moment he'd arrived back in town now raged nearly out of control inside him.

He slid his hands down her slender back and she seemed to meld against him, into him. Cupping her buttocks, he broke the kiss only long enough to trail kisses down her throat. She raised her face, allowing him better access to the hollow of her throat and although he'd thought it impossible, his desire for her increased.

It had been so achingly long since he'd been with her. It had been so long since he'd tasted the sweetness of her lips, stroked the silk of her skin, lost himself in her heat.

He stopped kissing her only long enough to sit on the edge of the bed and pull her down next to him, then he reclaimed her lips as they both fell backward on the soft, welcoming mattress.

He immediately rolled halfway on top of her,

relishing the feel of her bare legs against his, desperately wanting more.

Her nipples were visible despite the fact that she wore a bra and a tank top, and the sight of the pebbly hardness aroused him even more. He covered one of her breasts with his hand and rubbed his thumb against the turgid nipple. A deep, throaty moan issued from her.

Slow, he told himself. He wanted to take it slow although his body demanded immediate relief. He didn't want to hurry. He wanted to savor each caress, every kiss. He wanted to let her know through his touch that he wanted to be back in her life forever.

Slow, he thought again, but even as he told himself to slow down, his fingers pushed her tank top up above her lacy bra. Taking it slow was one thing, thoroughly torturing himself was quite another.

It had been over five long years since he'd last held her in his arms, five long years since he'd felt the splendor of her naked body against his. Take it slow be damned.

He sat up and quickly pulled his T-shirt over his head and threw it on the floor nearby. He then pulled her up and also took off her tank top, tossing it near his own shirt on the floor.

Her smoke-colored eyes were glazed as he wrapped his arms around her and once again lowered his mouth to hers. As he kissed her deeply, soulfully, his fingers unclasped the fastening of her bra and the garment slid away from her, leaving her half-naked in his arms.

Although words of love filled his head, begged to be released by his mouth, he kept his silence. She'd told him early in their marriage that she didn't like love talk, that she liked her lovemaking to take place in silence.

So, he bit back the words and instead spoke of his love and his passion with his actions. As his mouth moved down her neck, across her collarbone to her naked breast, her fingers tangled in his hair.

He felt her swift intake of breath as his tongue teased the rosy tip and her fingers tightened their grasp on his hair. He moved his fingers to the waistband of her jean shorts, his intention to unfasten them and sweep them down her long legs.

As his fingers touched the snap, her hand covered his and the glaze in her eyes cleared. She pushed against him and he immediately sat up.

"I'm sorry," she said as she crossed her arms over her naked breasts. "I…I'm not ready for this…I can't…"

"No, it's all right," he said despite the vast disappointment that swept through him. Too fast, he told himself. He'd tried to move things far too fast. "I don't want you to do anything that you don't want to do."

"I shouldn't have allowed things to go as far as

they did,'' she said, her cheeks pinked and her gaze averted from his.

"It's all right, Cookie…really.''

Awkwardly, she scooted past him and off the bed and quickly grabbed her bra and her tank top, then disappeared into the bathroom.

He grabbed his T-shirt and pulled it on, wondering how long he'd have to stand beneath a cold shower to douse the desire that still rocketed through his veins.

He should have known that it was too soon for lovemaking. He'd been back just a little over a week and in that time they'd had few occasions to recreate the bond they'd once had.

What he needed to do was romance his wife. He needed to court her, to bring back the magic they'd once had. He needed to make her fall in love with him all over again.


"I got pains where I didn't know I had body,'' Sarge complained as they finished up dinner that evening. Joshua had gone to get him soon after the scene in the bedroom and Claire had been grateful for the time alone to sort out her feelings where Joshua was concerned.

"That's good,'' Joshua said. "That means they were working muscles that needed to be worked.''

"Hmm, it's nothing more than a legal form of torture,'' Sarge replied.

Claire smiled and got up to begin clearing the

table. Sarge might be doing a lot of complaining, but his color was good and he seemed more animated than he had in weeks.

"I made arrangements for one of them fancy vans to pick me up in the mornings and take me to therapy, then bring me home in the afternoons," he continued. "Figured that way I wouldn't be putting anybody out, and besides, the folks at the hospital told me it was a free service."

"That's great, Sarge," Claire replied. "And now, why don't you two go on into the living room and let me clean up in here."

"Yeah, I'm ready for a little television," Sarge said.

Claire breathed a sigh of relief as the two men left her alone. She'd thought she'd been sensitive to Joshua's nearness in the past week, but since their afternoon intimacy, she was on edge as she hadn't been before.

Fortunately, Joshua hadn't pressed the issue when she'd come out of the bathroom after dressing, and within minutes, had left to get Sarge from the hospital.

Before she could get the table cleared off, Joshua returned to the kitchen. "Let me help," he said and picked up the last two remaining glasses.

"That's not necessary," she protested, not wanting to spend a second alone with him. At the moment she felt far too vulnerable.

He placed the glasses in the sink with the other

dirty dishes. "How about you rinse and I'll load the dishwasher?" he said.

What could she say? It would be churlish for her to reject his offer to help. She began rinsing off the dishes and handing them to him one at a time.

"I think it's a great sign that Sarge has arranged for his own transportation to and from the hospital," he said.

"It shows he's starting to think about a little independence."

"It will make it easier for me to work at City Hall without having to worry about getting him to and from therapy," she admitted, then added, "I worry about him, you know. He just hasn't been himself since the stroke."

She couldn't help but notice that each time Joshua took a dish from her his fingers seemed to linger a nanosecond too long on hers.

"Sarge is going to be just fine, Claire. He's a survivor. He'll get out of that wheelchair in no time now that he's going to therapy."

She nodded. All she wanted to do was get the dishes done and get out of the kitchen, away from Joshua's nearness.

However, even after they'd left the kitchen, his presence continued to disturb her peace of mind. As they watched television she felt his gaze lingering on her and when their eyes met, she saw desire shining from the depths of his.

She was more than grateful when Sarge asked

her to help him to bed. Once she got him settled in she would be able to escape to the privacy of her bedroom.

She helped Sarge into bed, then returned to the living room. "I think I'm going to call it a night, too," she said to Joshua, who had moved from a chair to the sofa.

He frowned, obviously disappointed. "So early? I thought maybe we could watch a movie together. You used to love watching movies in the evenings. I could pop some popcorn...extra butter," he cajoled.

How tempting it was to curl up on the sofa in his arms and watch a sappy movie while eating popcorn. How many nights had they spent doing that very thing when they'd first gotten married? A hundred?

"Thanks, but I'm really tired," she said. "Good night, Joshua."

"Good night, Claire." His voice held a wistful appeal that tugged at her heart, but she turned and raced down the hallway to her bedroom.

Once there, she undressed and pulled on her nightshirt, seeking the same kind of comfort from the familiar cotton material that she'd found that afternoon in his arms. But of course, the two couldn't really be compared.

She moved to the window and peered out at night falling. Deep-purple clouds chased across the sky, banishing the last of day's light.

Painfully, she contemplated the realization that she was still very much in love with her husband. Heaven help her, she didn't want to be. She'd been fighting against it from the moment she'd seen him standing at the Dragon Tree, attempting to dig up the treasure she sought.

She moved away from the window and sat on the edge of her bed, the same bed where she and Joshua had come precariously close to making love that afternoon.

She still loved Joshua—as deeply, as profoundly as she had over five years ago. When he'd left her, she'd believed her love had disappeared, died beneath the anguish of his desertion. But she'd been wrong.

It would have been so easy to give in to their lovemaking that afternoon, so easy to lose herself in her desire for him. But she knew that was the worst possible thing that could have happened.

She leaned forward and opened the drawer next to her bed and pulled out a small snapshot. It was a picture of the three of them—herself, Joshua and Sammy. Sammy was in one of Joshua's arms and his other arm was thrown around her shoulder.

It was a picture of a happy family. But the picture was outdated, for the happy family no longer existed. The little boy had died, the man had gone away and the woman had been left alone to cope with the bitter remains.

She traced a trembling finger over Sammy's little face, then drew her finger back as if it had been burned. She put the picture back in the drawer, unwilling to look at it for too long a time, afraid of the emotions staring at the picture might evoke in her.

Joshua had said that Sarge was a survivor and that was true. But she was a survivor, too. She'd survived the loss of her son and abandonment by her husband, and she had sworn that she would never again put herself in a position to suffer that kind of loss.

She knew that part of Joshua's dream for the future was children, and she had made the decision that there would be no more children in her life.

She didn't know what had driven him back here to Mayfield, but assumed it had to be loneliness and the fact that their marital status was, for all intents and purposes, in limbo. It was also obvious from the way he'd been acting that he wouldn't mind resuming their life as a married couple. But she couldn't do that.

Joshua had married her because she was pregnant, and when there was no more baby, there had been no more Joshua. Yes, she was still in love with her husband, but there was no way they'd ever share a future together.

She couldn't forget that he'd left her before and there was no guarantee that he wouldn't walk away from her again. And the next time she just might not survive.

# Chapter Eight

"I want to cook dinner for Sarge this evening and I'd like the two of you to get lost." Wilma Iverson looked at Joshua, then at Claire, her cheeks reddening as she waited for a reply.

Joshua was just grateful she didn't wink at him. They'd met earlier that morning as they'd both gone outside to get their papers and together had cooked up a scheme that might serve both their interests. Wilma wanted some quality time alone with Sarge, and Joshua wanted the same with Claire.

Claire frowned. "Sarge is so tired after his physical therapy sessions, I don't know if tonight..."

"I reckon he's got to eat whether he's tired or not," Wilma replied. "Now, all I'm asking is that the two of you let us old folks have a little time alone.''

She smoothed the skirt of her blue-flowered dress, then reached up to pat an errant gray hair into place. ''And I've got your evening all planned. I made reservations for the two of you down at the Onion Patch. And don't give me any nonsense about not going. I had to twist a few arms to get the table for you.''

Joshua eyed the older woman with surprise; she hadn't mentioned that she intended to arrange where he and Claire would go.

''The Onion Patch? I'm surprised that place is still open.''

''Still open and one of the most popular places in this one-horse town,'' Wilma replied. ''Most evenings it's almost impossible to get a table for dinner.''

Joshua looked at Claire. It was obvious from the expression on her face that she wasn't pleased with this turn of events. ''I don't think…'' she began.

''Oh, for heaven's sake, Claire. It's just a couple of hours,'' Wilma interjected before Claire could finish her protest. ''I've already gone to a lot of trouble to see that you and Joshua will be taken care of while I take care of your grandfather.''

Claire threw her hands in the air. ''All right.'' She looked from Wilma to Joshua. ''Then I suppose we'll go to the Onion Patch.''

''Good. I'll be over here about five to start cooking. I know Sarge likes to eat around six." Wilma picked up her purse from their kitchen table. "And now I'm off to the grocery store to pick up a few things. I'll see you two this evening."

"I told you I smelled a romance brewing," Joshua said when the front door had opened and closed, indicating that Wilma had left the house. He gestured toward Claire's empty glass. "Want some more iced tea?"

Joshua had been working out in the yard most of the morning and had come inside for a cold drink. He and Claire had been at the table when Wilma had arrived.

She shook her head. "No, thanks. I need to get back to work. I've got laundry to do and I want to change Sarge's sheets on his bed while he's gone."

"Need some help?"

"No." She got up from the table and placed her empty glass in the dishwasher. "I can't believe I'm being shoved out of my own home by my pushy next-door neighbor." Her nose wrinkled, a gesture Joshua remembered always indicated she was cranky.

"We don't have to go to the Onion Patch if you don't want to," he said. "We could just walk around downtown then get a bite to eat in the café."

She sighed, her frown deepening. "No, if I have to leave the house I might as well get something good to eat, and the Onion Patch has the best food in town. And now I've got to get to work.'' She left the kitchen and Joshua stared down into his iced tea.

Claire had been extremely distant and cool toward him from the moment she'd gotten out of bed that morning. He wanted to romance her, to court her, but it was difficult when she remained aloof.

Tonight he intended to tell her he still loved her with all his heart. Tonight he meant to tell her that he wanted the two of them to try again, to resolve their past issues and build a future together forever and always.

He just hoped that little wrinkle in her nose was gone by this evening. If she were cranky, she wouldn't want to hear anything he had to say to her. And what he wanted to say was too important for her not to listen. It wasn't just his feelings he wanted to talk about, it was the rest of his life.

*The rest of his life.* The words resounded in his head, mingling with the beat of his heart. He couldn't imagine the emptiness of his life without Claire.

He'd already wasted far too much time, allowing pride and anger and heartache to keep him away. It was past time to move on with the rest of his life and the only way he wanted to do it was with Claire at his side.

He worked in the yard until three that afternoon, then went inside to shower and prepare for the evening with Claire.

Sarge had gotten home a few minutes before and sat in the living room listening to talk radio. He turned his head as Joshua came into the room.

"I hear you two are leaving me at the hands of that woman next door tonight," he said.

"She wanted to cook dinner for you this evening," Joshua said. "I think she likes you, Sarge."

Sarge snorted. "What on earth could she like about a grouchy, old, half-crippled blind man?"

Joshua laughed. "I'd say that, despite all that, you have a certain charm about you. Would you rather Claire and I stay here?" Although Joshua didn't want to stay, he would never put Sarge in a position where he might be uncomfortable.

"Nah, I suppose I can tolerate Wilma for a few hours alone. Despite the fact that she can be opinionated and stubborn, she cooks like an angel, and I suppose she likes having somebody to fuss over. Besides, she can be good company. We remember the same things, come from the same era."

He didn't sound like a man who was dreading the night to come, Joshua thought with relief. "I'd better go get into the shower."

"Where are you and Cookie heading?"

"The Onion Patch."

Sarge nodded. "Good. As I recall, the two of you used to like to go out there and kick up your heels a bit." He nodded his head. "Dance with her, Joshua. Take her dancing and make her laugh."

"I'll do my best, Sarge," he said.

"You do better than that," the old man said with surprising firmness. "You love her, don't you?"

"More than anything or anyone else in the world." Speaking of his love for Claire aloud filled him with a rich elation. "I want it back, Sarge, the life we had. I want a future with her." Emotion welled up inside him, clogging his throat for a long moment. "I love her, Sarge, and I can't imagine a future without her."

"She needs you, boy. She might not know it, but she does. She hasn't been the same since you left here. Something broke inside her and I don't think anyone can fix it but you."

Sarge raked a hand through his thin white hair. "Life kicked you in the teeth when little Sammy died. You were just kids, not equipped to handle something as horrible as having to bury your child. I don't know exactly what happened to drive you two apart, but I do know that Cookie needs you now more than ever."

"I hope you're right," Joshua replied fervently.

Minutes later as Joshua stood beneath the shower spray, he thought of everything Sarge had said. Sarge seemed to think Claire needed him and Wilma had intimated the same. But Joshua wasn't sure about anything...especially not about what Claire had ever needed.

He fought a wave of guilt that washed over him.

Sarge's request that he take Claire out dancing and make her laugh was similar to what Wilma had said, that Claire had spent far too long a time cooped up in this house acting as caretaker.

If he hadn't left her all those years ago, he might have been here to help her cope, to ease her burden. Sure, in the years he'd been away he'd become a wealthy man, but no amount of money could replace the years she'd lost—the years *they* had lost.

He was suddenly struck by the fact that she hadn't had a phone call or a visit from a friend in the time he'd been here. What had happened to the girlfriends that had once called her daily, the friends she'd often met for lunch? He made a mental note to ask her about them.

He'd take her to the Onion Patch tonight; they'd dance on the old straw-strewn floor and eat the best steaks in the world. He'd tell her bad jokes, sing her silly ditties, do whatever it took to make those smoke-gray eyes of hers dance with laughter.

After they'd danced, and eaten and laughed, then he'd tell her his dream for their future. He hoped and he prayed that her dream was the same.

Although Claire tried to tell herself she didn't want to go out, that she was going to hate every moment spent in Joshua's company, the truth was that there was a tiny part of her that was looking forward to getting out of the house on a beautiful summer evening. Tonight would be a gift to herself. She would allow herself to enjoy being at the Onion Patch, she would have fun and not think of the past or the future.

She frowned at her reflection in the mirror, an ache piercing her at this thought. She'd married Joshua with the desire for the two of them to enjoy a happily-ever-after. But Sammy's death and Joshua's desertion had changed everything. She no longer looked for a happily-ever-after.

She shoved these thoughts away and focused on her appearance. She'd chosen to wear a turquoise sundress. The neckline was square-cut, the bodice was fitted and the skirt was flared, ending at her knees. Her hair was braided down her back and tiny gold hoops decorated her dainty earlobes.

As she turned away from the dresser, her gaze fell on the tin box that contained the photo of Sarah and Daniel. An impulse to open the box and take out the picture swept over her, but she ignored it.

She was half-afraid to look at it again, knowing that it was possible it might have changed yet once more. She no longer asked herself how it was possible that an old photograph could transform itself.

She didn't know how it was possible, she only knew that it was. And somehow she had begun to believe that the photo was a reflection of her relationship with Joshua.

When they had first found the photo, on the day that Joshua had arrived back in Mayfield, the couple in the picture had shown an emotional distance from one another. Then, when she'd gotten the feeling that Joshua still cared for her, when she'd seen the look of desire shining from his eyes, the photo had changed to reflect the same thing in Daniel's posture and expression.

She didn't want to look at the picture again because she feared she'd see her own love for Joshua shining from Sarah's eyes where it hadn't been before. As crazy as it sounded, she didn't want a magic picture to confirm what she felt in her heart for Joshua.

A knock sounded on her bedroom door. "Yes?"

"Wilma is here. Are you ready to go?" Joshua's strong voice came through the closed door.

"I'm ready." She grabbed her purse from the bed then opened the door to see him standing there.

Her breath momentarily caught in her throat at the sight of him. He wore a pair of navy dress slacks and a light-blue short-sleeve dress shirt. The color of the shirt intensified the green of his eyes and accented the darkness of his hair. He looked as handsome as she'd ever seen him.

"You look beautiful, Cookie," he said softly, his eyes caressing her with a heated gaze.

"Why, thank you, sir. You clean up right nice, too," she said with a forced lightness of tone.

As they walked down the hallway, she could hear the clang of pots and pans coming from the kitchen and Wilma chattering about a recipe she'd seen on a television cooking program.

"We're leaving," Claire said as they entered the kitchen where Wilma bustled from the counter to the stove and Sarge sat at the kitchen table, a bemused expression on his face.

He raised a hand and nodded. "Have fun."

"And don't worry about a thing here," Wilma said. "I've got a gourmet meal planned for the two of us and after dinner I brought some tapes of some old radio shows I thought we might listen to."

She apparently had the entire night planned, Claire thought in surprise and realized Joshua had been right. It seemed that Wilma had set her cap for Sarge.

Murmuring their goodbyes, Joshua and Claire left the house. Joshua's car awaited them in the driveway. Joshua opened the passenger door for her and she slid in, then watched as he walked around the front of the car to the driver's door.

The last thing she wanted to be doing was going to the Onion Patch with Joshua, but because Wilma had made the arrangements it had been difficult for Claire to say no.

Surely she could enjoy the evening despite the company she kept, she told herself.

He slid behind the wheel, bringing with him the evocative scent that made her pulse beat just a little bit faster than normal. She fastened her seat belt as he pulled out of the driveway and headed toward the north edge of town.

"I was surprised when Wilma said she'd made reservations for us at the Onion Patch," he said. "I figured the place would have closed down long ago."

She smiled. "It's the only place to go to dance and hear live music."

"Does Freddy still own it?"

"Freddy is as much a fixture as the onions he's got hanging from the ceiling," she replied.

"He was always good about letting us come in even though we were underage," Joshua said.

"But he would have killed us if he'd ever caught us with a drink in our hands."

"You've got that right," Joshua said with a laugh. "And he had the reputation that made me think he could kill us without blinking an eye."

"I think Freddy's reputation is all of his own making." She felt herself relaxing with the innocuous topic of conversation. "He has all those awful-looking tattoos and he's big as a horse, but for as long as he's lived in town, nobody has ever had any problems with him."

She relaxed even more as he began asking her about other people in town. "What about Susan Kelly? The two of you used to be really tight. What happened to her?" he asked.

"She married some guy from Kansas City and

moved there. We still write occasionally to each other.''

"What about Melinda? You two were best friends, but you haven't mentioned her while I've been back.''

"Actually, last I heard she was waitressing at the Onion Patch," Claire said, fighting against a wave of nostalgia as she thought of the woman who had been her best friend since they'd been in third grade. "I don't see much of her anymore. You know how it is. As people get older and busier, it gets more difficult to maintain the friendships of youth.''

She stared out the window, for a moment her thoughts consumed with Melinda. When Sammy had passed away, Melinda had been carrying her first child and the distance between Melinda and Claire had grown too great to breach. Just another loss, Claire thought sadly, just another loss in a list of many.

The Onion Patch was a long, flat wooden building with a gaudy neon sign that proclaimed the name of the establishment. It had been named for the field where it had been built, a large garden where the main crop had been onions.

Even though it was early, there were already several cars and trucks parked in the immense parking area in front of the building. Raucous country-and-western music spilled from the open doorway, and the scent of grilled meat and onions filled the air.

As they walked across the parking lot, Joshua threw an arm around Claire's shoulders. She thought about walking out of the casual embrace, then chided herself. It wasn't as if he was pulling her into his arms or pressing intimately against her.

Once inside they were greeted by Freddy, who shook Joshua's hand vigorously and wrapped Claire in a bear hug. ''I couldn't believe it when Wilma Iverson called and wanted to reserve a table for the two of you,'' the big man exclaimed. ''My favorite video game is one of yours,'' he said to Joshua.

''Really? Which one?''

''Captain Cool's Castle,'' Freddy said. ''Except I haven't been able to get past that goofy-looking monster on the fourth level.''

Joshua laughed. ''Look behind a flower vase on the third level and you'll find the weapon to destroy the goofy-looking monster.''

''Great, thanks,'' Freddy exclaimed as he led them through the dark interior to a familiar table in the back.

It was the table where the two of them had spent many evenings when they were first married and Claire had been pregnant with Sammy and life was good.

Before Claire sat down and as Freddy was walking away, Melinda appeared at the table. She squealed a greeting then pulled Claire into a hug. "Oh, gosh, girl. It's so good to see you!" Melinda exclaimed as she released Claire. "You look great!" She turned her attention to Joshua and hugged him, as well. "I heard you were back in town."

"It's good to see you, too, Melinda," Joshua said.

Melinda grabbed Claire by the hand. "You'll excuse us for a minute, won't you?" Without giving Joshua a chance to reply, Melinda pulled Claire across the dance floor and into the women's rest room.

"Claire, it's been too long." Melinda grabbed Claire's hands and peered into her eyes.

"It has," Claire agreed, surprised to feel a ball of emotion press thick inside her chest.

"We've let the years get away from us and we shouldn't have."

Claire nodded. "How's John? And your daughter?" She was appalled to realize she didn't even know Melinda's little girl's name.

"Good. John is great, although we don't see much of each other these days. He works days and I stay home with Rebecca, then I work nights and he takes care of her. We're saving for a house. We're sick of apartment living. What about you? How's Sarge?"

"He's fine, as ornery as ever."

"And Joshua...are the two of you..."

"No," Claire said hurriedly. "He's just in town visiting."

"He's still quite a hunk, isn't he?"

"Yeah, I guess so," Claire replied.

"How about we get together for lunch next week?" Melinda asked.

"I'd like that." Claire smiled. "And now I guess I'd better get out there." She turned to leave, but stopped as Melinda called her name once again.

"I know it's been a long time— I've always felt as if I somehow let you down." Melinda's expression was troubled.

"Let me down?" Claire looked at her in surprise. "How?"

"I wasn't really there for you when Sammy died. I tried to be, but I felt like you preferred to be alone in your grief. Maybe I should have tried harder to be there for you."

"It was a long time ago," Claire said softly. "And you're here now and we'll have lunch and catch up on everything that has happened since we last talked."

Melinda brightened. "I've missed you, Claire."

"I've missed you, too. Call me." With these final words, Claire left the rest room and hurried back to the table where Joshua awaited her.

"I was beginning to think you might have slipped out the back door," he said as she sat next to him.

"I thought about it, but then realized you'd probably tattle to Wilma and she'd be cranky with me for the next month."

He laughed. "The last thing I'd want is to have Wilma Iverson mad at me."

Before she could say anything, their waitress appeared at the table to take their dinner orders. After she'd departed, Claire found herself thinking about Sarge and Wilma. In all the years that she'd been with Sarge, he'd never dated or shown any interest in any member of the opposite sex.

Claire's grandmother had died the year before Claire's parents had passed away and once Claire had arrived at Sarge's house, he'd devoted his all to raising her.

"You're awfully quiet," Joshua said.

"I was just thinking about Sarge and Wilma."

"What about them?"

She picked up her water glass and took a sip, grateful that the jukebox was momentarily silent. "I was just thinking about the fact that it's far past time for Sarge to enjoy the company of a woman his age. He's been alone for a very long time, too long."

"Sarge will require some extra attention because of his blindness, but Wilma doesn't seem daunted by it. I think she's a woman who needs to take care of somebody."

"I think you're right," Claire replied. At that

moment the jukebox began to play a foot-stompin',
heart-stoppin' tune and the two of them fell silent.

While Claire was thrilled with the prospect that
Sarge might enjoy a romance with Wilma, she was
also aware that if Wilma moved into his life, Claire
would need to move out of it a bit.

Without the job of caretaking for Sarge, she recognized that her life would be empty, lonely. She
shoved this thought away as the waitress appeared
once again with their drink order.

As the minutes ticked by and she and Joshua
sipped their beer, the place began to fill with more
and more people from town. Before long, they
were visiting with neighbors who stopped by their
table to say hello and Claire found herself relaxing
despite the fact that she'd initially not wanted to
come.

Their meals came and they ate while talking
about everything from old movies to world poli-
tics. They seemed to have a mutual agreement to
steer clear of any topic that was too close, any
subject that might create tension.

By the time they'd finished their meals and ordered a second beer, the band had begun to warm
up and the place was packed. "Come on, let's
dance," Joshua said as the band began its first
tune.

Claire hesitated only a minute. She'd always
loved to dance and she'd always loved to dance

with Joshua, who was a strong lead and made her feel as if she were floating on air.

Besides, even though she hadn't wanted to come here with Joshua, she was here now and she decided just to enjoy herself.

Their first dance was a fast one. The dance floor was crowded, but the band was good and she threw herself into allowing the music to take possession of her.

When the fast dance was over the band segued into a slow tune and before she could protest, Joshua took her into his arms.

Initially, she held herself stiff, unyielding, but it didn't take long for her to give in to the sweet sensation of being held in his arms.

Their dancing together was as familiar to her as their lovemaking. There were no awkward movements, no stumbling on toes. They moved as one, and in the beauty of their dancing, an edge of bitterness once again rose up inside her.

They might have danced through life together, moving in perfect sync through joys and sorrows, if he hadn't walked away from her.

# Chapter Nine

Joshua had intended to finish up the evening by telling Claire that he was still in love with her, that he wanted to spend the rest of his life with her. But as the evening wore on he realized that perhaps tonight wasn't the time to do such a thing.

Things had been going so well. She'd been relaxed and smiling and had seemed happy until they'd danced a slow dance. He'd felt the change in her body before he'd seen it on her face. She'd stiffened with tension.

When the dance had ended and they returned to their table, she was quiet, her expression cool and aloof. He tried to get back the comradery and warmth they had shared over their meal, but she remained distant and unwilling to engage emotionally with him.

It was just before ten when she indicated she wanted to go home, and he did nothing to attempt to change her mind. They rode back to the house in an uncomfortable silence. Several times he attempted to make conversation, but she had withdrawn deep into a place where he couldn't seem to reach her.

A small wave of despair swept through him, then he told himself that perhaps he was expecting too much too soon. He'd been gone for five years and back in her life for less than two weeks. But his love for her made him impatient, eager to get on with the rest of their lives.

"I hope we don't catch Sarge and Wilma smooching on the sofa," he said as he pulled into the driveway.

Claire flashed him a horrified look. "You don't think that's what they're doing, do you?"

He grinned at her. "Why wouldn't they be doing that? They're legal age and if they feel affection for each other, why wouldn't they express that affection?" He shut off the engine and turned to look at her.

As always, the sight of her hit him square in the stomach like a hard punch. It had been that way the very first time he'd seen her when they had been so young. He'd taken one look at her thick-lashed gray eyes, the stubborn thrust of her chin and her lush, full lips, and he'd been a goner.

Even now, with that wrinkle of annoyance along the side of her nose, and a line of distraction across her forehead, he felt that force of love hit hard in the pit of his stomach.

"What's wrong, Cookie?" he asked softly. "Something happened at the Onion Patch that upset you." He reached out a hand and placed it over hers.

She turned her gaze from the house to him and pulled her hand away. "Nothing's wrong. I'm just tired, that's all. It's been a long day."

He knew it was more than that, but he didn't know how to breach the walls she'd erected around herself...the same walls she'd erected when Sammy had died.

The distancing he felt from her now was the same that had eventually driven him out of their house, out of her life. An edge of frustration pulled forth a tiny stir of anger that he quickly tamped down.

They got out of the car and walked to the house. He stopped her on the porch by touching her arm, attempting one last time to connect with her. She turned to look at him, her eyes dark and mysterious.

"You want to sit for a minute on the porch swing?" he asked. "It's a beautiful night."

"No. I just want to get settled in."

He wanted to pull her down into the porch swing, where they had spent so many nights talking and sharing and kissing in the past. He wanted somehow to force her to talk to him, to open up. But he didn't.

He followed her into the house where Wilma and Sarge were seated on the sofa, a recording of "The Shadow" playing on the stereo.

"You're back," Wilma announced the obvious and jumped up to turn off the tape of the old radio show.

"You two have a good time?" Sarge asked.

"Fine," Claire replied curtly.

"What about the two of you?" Joshua asked.

"We managed," Sarge replied.

"We did more than manage," Wilma protested. "It was a lovely evening and you know it, Samuel Cook."

Sarge grinned. "If you say so, Wilma."

"Well, I do say so. And now I'll just gather my things and head on home," Wilma said.

She disappeared into the kitchen and returned a moment later with her purse and a plastic bag in her hands. "There's some leftover spaghetti and meatballs in the refrigerator if you all get hungry. Sarge, don't forget that as soon as you can get out of that wheelchair you and I have a date down at the Onion Patch."

"You got it," he said. "We'll show those young folks how to cut a rug on the dance floor."

Murmuring goodbye, Wilma left. "Are you ready for bed?" Claire asked Sarge.

"Not really. I need a bit of time to unwind." He directed his sightless gaze in the direction of Claire's voice. "But if you're tired, go on to bed. Joshua can help me when I'm ready."

"Sure, no problem," Joshua replied. He wasn't ready for bed yet either. He wanted to think, to assess the evening and see if he could figure out what had happened to transform Claire.

"Then I'll just say good-night," Claire said and disappeared down the hallway to her room.

"I see you managed to get out of your chair," Joshua said as he sat next to Sarge on the sofa.

"Yeah. Took nearly all my energy, but Wilma helped me and we managed to get me here on the sofa. It's a little cozier to sit with a woman on a sofa than to sit in a wheelchair next to the sofa."

"So, you really had a good time?"

"That woman talks faster than a used-car salesman," Sarge said gruffly, but there was a touch of affection in his voice. "But yeah, I had a good time. What about you? I could tell by Cookie's voice that things didn't go so well for the two of you."

Joshua leaned back and raked a hand through his hair in frustration. "I don't know what happened, Sarge. Things seemed to go pretty well at first. We ate dinner and talked...she seemed relaxed and happy. Everything appeared to be going fine. Then we danced and everything changed.''

''What did you do? Step on her toes?''

''I didn't step on her toes, but she sure closed up and turned off. She hardly looked at me for the rest of the night.''

Sarge frowned. ''I can't help you with this one, son. For most of my life I've found women difficult to comprehend. They think different than we do, feel different, too.''

''There's just one woman in this world I want to understand, and that's Claire,'' Joshua said softly.

''Maybe a little patience is in order,'' Sarge suggested. ''You were gone a long time, Joshua.''

''Too long,'' Joshua exclaimed.

For an endless moment the two men were silent. Again Joshua found himself trying to figure out why Claire had withdrawn from him, but no answers came to mind.

''The games I create are so easy,'' Joshua finally said. ''In my games I can program my characters to do whatever I want them to do.''

''Claire isn't a character in one of your games and you can't make her do what you want by clicking a mouse.''

''I know,'' Joshua replied with a sigh of renewed frustration.

There was a long moment of silence between

them. "Maybe I raised her too tough," Sarge finally said.

Joshua looked at him curiously. "What do you mean?"

"She probably needed a woman's touch in her life, a female influence of sorts. I was tough on her, didn't like to see her cry. I don't know," he finally finished tiredly. "I think I'm ready for bed now."

Joshua got up and helped Sarge into his wheelchair, then pushed him down the hallway into his bedroom. It took only moments to get him into his pajamas and into bed.

"Goodnight, Sarge."

"Don't give up too easily, Joshua," Sarge said softly. "There are some couples who are just destined to be together, and I always believed you and Claire were like that. If she's your soul mate, Joshua, then don't give up on her too damned easily."

A half an hour later, Joshua sat on the porch swing, listening to the symphony of night that surrounded him. Sarge's words played and replayed in his head.

On the first day he'd seen Claire, he'd known that she was his soul mate, the woman with whom he was supposed to spend his life...eternity and beyond.

Had he been wrong? Was Sarge wrong? Was it

possible that he and Claire were not soul mates at
all, but had been destined to share only a brief
moment in their lives?

She awoke with tears on her cheeks. Shocked,
Claire sat up in bed and swiped them away. It had
been years and years since she'd last cried actual
tears. The last time she could remember was when
she'd been eight and a policewoman had gently
told her that her parents had died in a car accident
and had gone to heaven.

When Sammy had died, her grief had been too
huge for tears. As much as she'd wanted to weep,
had felt the need to weep, her eyes had remained
painfully dry.

She frowned, but no matter how hard she tried
she couldn't remember exactly what dream images
had invoked these tears. Lying back down, she
glanced at the clock and noted it was just after six,
far too early to get out of bed. She didn't want to
get up and have to spend time alone in Joshua's
company.

It was obvious to her that he was doing everything in his power to romance her, seduce her back
into a relationship with him. But she had to remain
strong. She had to guard her heart against him.

It didn't matter that his touch still made her heart
sing, that his nearness made her pulse beat faster.
It didn't matter that he could make her laugh as
nobody had before or since him. All of that was

negated by the fact that he'd deserted her and she couldn't risk her heart to him again.

She remained in bed until seven, knowing Sarge would be awake at any moment. Then she got up, showered, dressed and steeled herself to face another day with Joshua in the house.

At least she could leave for her new job at City Hall by eight-thirty and spend a couple of hours there while Sarge was at his physical therapy session.

When she went into the kitchen she was surprised to see Sarge already seated at the table eating breakfast. Joshua stood at the stove and he turned to flash her a quick smile.

"Good morning. I was just making myself a couple of eggs. Want me to fry you up a couple?"

"No, thanks. Coffee is fine for me." She poured herself a cup of coffee and sat next to Sarge at the table. "You sleep okay, Sarge?" she asked.

"Like a log. What about you?"

"I slept all right. Don't forget that while you're at therapy today, I'll be working down at City Hall for a couple of hours."

"And while you're working there, I'm going to do a little searching for that treasure you're after," Joshua said as he moved from the stove to the table. He set his plate on the table and sat.

She looked at him in surprise. "Have you thought of where it might be buried?"

"No place specific," he replied. "I just thought

I'd walk around and look for places where the clues might fit.'' His gaze held hers for a long moment. ''I know how important finding it is to you.''

She nodded, but was surprised to realize that in the last week she'd hardly thought of the treasure. She'd been so consumed with thoughts of Sarah and Daniel Walker and so caught up in her emotions where Joshua was concerned, she'd scarcely remembered that somewhere in the town of Mayfield was a buried treasure that was supposed to change her life.

The three of them small-talked for a bit, then Claire excused herself to get ready for work. As she left the house, she suddenly remembered that she'd dreamed something about Daniel and Sarah. She couldn't remember what the dream had been, but whatever it was, it had made her cry.

She walked briskly toward City Hall, her thoughts filled with Joshua. His presence in her home, in her life, was becoming more and more difficult for her. He was making her remember all the reasons she'd fallen in love with him. And she didn't want to remember them. She wanted, needed to remember how she'd felt when he'd left her.

It was easy to lose herself in the basement of City Hall amid the records of the past. Clark Windsloe had prepared a large work table with a computer and scanner down there for her.

She picked up a box she hadn't been through yet and began work. She scanned and catalogued and read, studying each piece of the past. Particularly interesting to her were the personal letters and diaries the box contained.

She worked until just after noon and was about to call it a day when she ran across a diary entry that horrified her. She had no idea who had written it, as the name on the front of the diary was no longer legible. The entry was dated June 2, 1859.

''Overcast day. Appropriate for a funeral, I suppose,'' the author had penned.

Too many funerals lately. The influenza has taken both the very old and the young. Today we buried little Caleb Walker. It broke my heart to see Daniel and Sarah grieve so, but at least they have each other to cling to.

Claire slammed the diary shut, chills racing up her spine as she suddenly remembered the dream she'd had the night before. She'd dreamed of the funeral. Daniel and Sarah had stood at the side of a tiny grave, their arms wrapped around each other as grief ripped through them.

Caleb had died.

Thick emotion pressed tightly against her chest, half suffocating her as she shut down the power on the computer, then raced from the basement.

She needed to get home. She felt sick to her stomach, frightened by the emotions that raced through her. She told herself what she was feeling was the strange connection with Daniel and Sarah, that it was their grief that created the metallic taste of despair in the back of her throat.

She was grateful she met no one on her way home, grateful that she didn't need to appear pleasant or engage in small talk. She just wanted the privacy of her bedroom, needed to lie down and let the crazy feelings roiling around inside her quiet down.

To her dismay, Joshua was in the front yard weeding a flower bed. He straightened as she approached and she saw the alarm that swept over his features. "Claire, what's wrong?"

She shook her head, dismissing his question and raced for the front door. Alone. She needed to be alone to deal with this tragedy. Breathing a trembling sigh, she reached her bedroom, but was surprised to find Joshua immediately behind her.

"Joshua…please…I need to be alone…" His face blurred and she realized her eyes were filled with tears that begged to be released. She turned away, but he stopped her by grabbing her forearm.

"Tell me what's wrong, Claire," he said, his voice betraying worry. "What happened?"

She tried to pull away from him, but he held tight. "Please…just let me go," she begged, hot tears now burning her cheeks.

"No, not until you tell me what's going on," he exclaimed.

"He's dead." The words exploded from her

along with a choked sob. Again she tried to yank away from him, frustrated when he refused to relinquish his hold on her.

"Who's dead?" His hand tightened on her arm. "Did something happen to Sarge?"

"No...Caleb...Caleb is dead." She half screamed the words and stumbled backward as he finally let go of her.

He raked a hand through his hair, his eyes displaying confusion. "Caleb? Who the hell is Caleb?"

She sank down on the edge of her bed, her legs unable to hold her upright another minute. "Caleb Walker. Sarah and Daniel's son. He's dead, Joshua. He died."

He sat down next to her on the bed, his expression still one of confusion. "Of course he's dead, Cookie," he said gently. "Caleb Walker lived a very long time ago."

She shook her head vehemently, aware that he didn't understand. "No...he died when he was just two years old...I saw the funeral. I feel Sarah and Daniel's pain and it hurts. Oh, God, Joshua, it hurts so badly."

Sobs clawed at her throat and she started to turn away from him, horrified that he would see her like this, terrified because she couldn't stop the wrenching cries that came from her along with the flood of tears.

He didn't allow her to turn away. He wrapped

his arms around her and pulled her against his chest. For a moment she fought him, believing what she wanted more than anything was privacy and the inner strength to pull herself together. She felt stupid, weak. It was ridiculous for her to fall apart over the death of a little boy a century and a half ago, a little boy she'd never known.

But Joshua fought, too, holding on to her until she collapsed against him, deep sobs ripping through her.

"It's all right," he murmured softly as he stroked her hair. "Go ahead and cry, Claire. Cry for Caleb."

And she did. She clung to him and wept as she couldn't remember crying before. Each time she thought the tears were depleted, a new round gripped her, leaving her weak and gasping in Joshua's arms.

"It's not fair," she sobbed and buried her face in the broad expanse of his warm chest. "He was just a little boy."

"I know…I know, baby." Joshua's eyes misted as a depth of emotion rose up in him. "It's okay to cry, Claire. Cry for Caleb. Cry for Sammy."

It was then she realized her tears were not for Sarah and Daniel's child, but rather for her own. It had taken her five long years, but she was finally crying for her son.

# Chapter Ten

Joshua hadn't been fooled. He knew from the moment she'd begun to cry that Claire's tears weren't for a little boy who had died well over a hundred years before. He'd known instantly that she wept for little Sammy and the emptiness his death had left behind.

As Claire cried, Joshua wept, too, his heart filled with pain for himself and for Claire. When her sobs subsided, leaving behind tiny hiccuping gasps, he laid her back on the bed but kept her in his arms.

After a few minutes she fell asleep, apparently exhausted by the torrent of emotions she'd experienced. He watched her sleep, grateful that he'd been here to hold her while she'd finally grieved for the son they'd lost, grateful that they'd finally had the chance to hold one another.

He frowned, thinking back to those days and weeks after Sammy had left them. While he'd railed and sobbed, drunk and cussed, Claire had remained dry-eyed and stoic. She'd thrown herself into housecleaning, cooking elaborate meals, grocery shopping and taking ceramic classes at the community center.

He'd wanted to talk about Sammy, try to figure out why this had happened to them. But she'd refused to talk to him about anything to do with Sammy. In fact, she'd stopped talking to him altogether, stopped touching him, stopped making love with him.

For the first month he told himself that eventually she'd come back to him, that there would come a time when she'd reach for him with need, with passion, with love. But days had passed, weeks, then months and he'd begun to die inside.

It was then he'd realized he had to leave. There was simply no reason to stay. Whatever good had existed between them had apparently been buried with Sammy.

Claire slept for less than an hour, then began to stir. She opened her reddened, slightly swollen eyes and sat up. "I...I'm sorry." She averted her gaze from his. "I...I can't believe I did that."

He smiled. "I can't believe it took you this long to do that. Claire..." He took hold of her chin, forcing her to look at him. "You shouldn't be ashamed or embarrassed about crying."

She nodded. "I just can't believe finding out about Caleb Walker made me lose it like that." She moved away from him and stood. "I've got to get busy." She looked around in distraction.

"Before you do, there's something I want to show you." He got up off the bed. "Come with me."

He led her down the hallway to the bedroom where he had been staying. "What?" she asked, hesitating on the threshold.

"Come. Sit." He gestured toward the bed and grabbed his laptop computer from the top of the dresser.

With a look of bewilderment, she did as he bid, sitting on the edge of the bed. He sat next to her and placed the compact computer on his lap, then turned it on.

"When I first learned to program computer games, I made up one just for myself, not for commercial use." The computer whirred and clicked as it loaded, sounds that had become as familiar to him as his own heartbeat. "It will probably seem stupid to you, but playing it always brought me a dose of comfort."

She said nothing, but watched curiously as he quickly typed in a series of commands. The screen went black for a moment, then filled with a series of white dancing stars that formed the words, Sammy Gets His Wings.

He heard her utter a soft gasp and for a moment thought she might get up and leave. But she remained beside him, leaning close, her features a mixture of dread and reluctant curiosity.

The title disappeared and a little boy's face appeared, a little boy who looked remarkably like Sammy. "The object of the game is to get Sammy to heaven where he gets his angel wings," he said softly. "During the journey he encounters a number of obstacles, but he has two helpmates along the way."

"His mother and his father," Claire said in a whisper.

He nodded and pulled up the two characters.

Again she gasped. "They look just like us."

"Well, as good as computer images can look," he replied. Using the touchpad, he quickly worked through the game as she watched. "I made it very easy. It was important to me that every time I played it, I won."

Within seconds he'd reached the end of the game and wings appeared on Sammy's back. With a beatific smile, the computer Sammy waved. "Goodbye Mommy, goodbye Daddy. I'll be waiting for you in heaven," he said.

The screen went blank, but Joshua continued to stare at it. "I can't tell you how many nights I played this game. It always made me feel bet-

ter…close to Sammy and close to you.'' He finally
turned to look at her and saw tears shining in her
eyes once again.

''It's beautiful, Joshua.'' Her gaze held his intently. ''Do you really believe Sammy is in
heaven?''

''Without a doubt,'' he replied firmly, then
smiled. ''He and Caleb Walker are probably great
friends. I'll bet if we listen real hard we could hear
them giggling as they wreak havoc in heaven, the
way only two little boys can.''

She smiled and he recognized the smile of a
woman finally at peace. He knew that there would
always be a piece of their hearts that would retain
the painful loss of their son, but whether it was her
tears for Sammy or the thought of him in heaven,
there was definitely a shine of resigned peace in
her eyes.

Just as he had known that now had been the time
to show her his game, he also knew that now was
the time to tell her of his love.

''Claire,'' he began and placed the laptop on the
bed next to him. ''I want it back, Cookie.'' He took
her hands in his. ''I want our life back. I love you.
I've never stopped loving you and I need us to be
together again.''

Whatever it had been he'd hoped to see on her
face, in her eyes, it wasn't there. Pain etched its
way across her features as she pulled her hands

from his. "You don't know what you're asking," she said and stood.

"I'm asking you to be my wife again, for us to have more children together, spend our days and nights together, grow old together."

"I can't do that." Her eyes were dark once again, haunted. "We had our chance at happiness, Joshua, and it wasn't in our cards."

"But it could be!" he exclaimed fervently. "I know you still love me, Cookie." He leaned toward her. "It's in your eyes when you look at me. I tasted it in your kisses. Give us a chance to get it right."

"I can't." Her voice rang with a slight hint of bitterness and she drew a deep breath. "You left me, Joshua. We had lost our son and you walked out on me." Her eyes flashed with anger. "You left me alone and I can't forget that."

"You were alone before I left," he said curtly, surprised to find his own anger rising up inside him. "I didn't walk out, you froze me out."

"Don't be ridiculous," she scoffed and rose and walked out of his bedroom.

He followed behind her, recognizing somewhere in the back of his mind that his anger was quickly spinning out of control. He was also aware of the fact that it wasn't an anger bred of this moment, but rather one that had been born on the day he'd left five years before.

"It isn't ridiculous, Claire," he said as they entered the living room. "You pushed me out of your life. You wouldn't talk to me, cry with me. Hell, you wouldn't even make love with me." In an instant, all the emotions he'd felt at that time came back, the despair, the frustration and the aching loneliness.

"At the time, that's not what I needed from you." Her voice was shriller than he'd ever heard it and he realized this was what was needed between them, a clearing of the air, a naked display of emotions that just might make them stronger in the end.

"Then what did you need from me, Claire?" He ran a hand through his hair and stared at her. Even with his anger, even with her own anger, in the back place of his heart he wanted nothing more than to gather her in his arms and make everything in both their worlds right again. "For God's sake, please tell me what you needed from me."

"Nothing." She looked away from him, the anger in her voice gone. "I just needed you to let me deal with things my own way, but I didn't need you to abandon me and I can't—I won't forgive you for that."

Joshua felt something die inside him as he heard her say what he'd always believed, that she hadn't needed him. He hadn't realized until this moment how desperately he'd needed her to need him.

"You don't play fair, Cookie. You shove me out of your life, then you're angry because I leave."

He'd been wrong, this clearing of the air between them hadn't helped them. He feared it had just destroyed them.

"I'm finished talking about this," she said stiffly.

"Don't worry, I'm done." He headed for the front door. "I'm going for a walk. I need some fresh air. But think about this—maybe you didn't need me, but did you ever think about the fact that I might have needed you?"

He didn't wait for her reply. He left the house, a grief such as he'd never known before weighing heavy in his heart. Initially, when Sammy had died, he'd grieved long and hard, but believed he'd have the comfort of Claire at his side.

Even in the five years he'd been away, Claire had never been out of his heart, out of his thoughts. He realized now that deep in his heart, he'd hoped they'd get back together and fulfill the future he believed destiny had mapped for them.

He didn't stop walking until he reached the city square, then he sank onto a stone bench beneath a leafy shade tree and buried his head in his hands.

He'd always believed he'd walked away from Claire because he'd wanted her to need him. But now he was faced with the truth of the matter. He'd walked away because he'd needed her so badly and she hadn't been there for him. He'd walked away because he'd been too weak to stay.

\* \* \*

As soon as he walked out the front door, Claire went back to her bedroom and sank down on the edge of her bed. She was exhausted, first from her crying jag and then from the emotional outburst with Joshua.

Joshua. Her heart cried as her mind replayed his words. *I love you…I need us to be together again.* But for how long? Until the next tragedy struck their lives? For life was made of triumphs and tragedies, and any couple that shared their lives experienced both.

He'd walked away from her before and she couldn't believe that he wouldn't again. As much as she loved him, as much as she wished she could believe in him again, she couldn't.

It was funny, she'd thought that the reason she wouldn't share a future with Joshua was that she had intended never to have children again.

But her tears for Sammy had swept away the fear in her heart. Loving Sammy and grieving for him had opened her heart to the possibility of more children in her life. She had a wealth of love to give and the memory of Sammy now merely served to strengthen her desire to have another child.

Still, she couldn't let go of her anger where Joshua was concerned. As she got up from the bed, her gaze fell on the tin box that held the picture of Sarah and Daniel.

She didn't want to look at it, didn't want to see

if the picture had transformed itself yet again. And yet, she couldn't not look.

Her fingers trembled as she opened the box and withdrew the photo. For a moment she didn't look at it, but simply held it in her hands, feeling the electrical currents that emanated from it.

She'd come to believe that the photo somehow mirrored her and Joshua's emotions. Would it now show Sarah all alone? Had the death of Caleb Walker torn Sarah and Daniel apart just as Sammy's death had ripped apart her and Joshua's marriage?

For some reason she knew that if she looked at the picture and saw Sarah all alone, a little piece of herself would die.

She lowered her gaze and gasped. Sarah wasn't alone. She and Daniel stood together and in front of them were two children, a boy about eight years old and a girl who looked to be about six.

Claire threw the picture across the room as tears sprang to her eyes. It was as if the photo mocked her, showing her a picture of the happy family she would never have.

There was no magic in that picture. It was simply a cruel trick to break her heart once again.

She got up and left the bedroom, refusing to cry over Joshua. He'd made his decision to walk out of her life five years before and now she was making her choice to keep him out of her life forever.

She needed action. She began unloading the clean dishes from the dishwasher, trying desperately to keep her mind a calm blank. But the conversation with Joshua refused to stay quiet.

*I didn't walk out, you froze me out.*

*You don't play fair. You shove me out of your life then you're angry because I leave.*

The words he'd said to her played and replayed in her mind. She hadn't done that, had she? He was just looking to place blame on her shoulders instead of accepting the consequences of what he'd done.

But, hadn't Melinda said something in the same vein to her last night in the rest room? Something about wanting to comfort her, but getting the impression that Claire wanted only to be alone?

She shoved these disturbing thoughts aside, refusing to dwell on them. She finished putting the dishes away, then made herself a glass of iced tea and sat outside on the porch swing.

She wondered where Joshua had gone and how much longer he'd be staying. Now that he knew there was nothing left for him here, surely he'd go back to California. He'd leave again, only this time he'd never return. Wasn't that what she wanted?

Rubbing her forehead, she realized she'd never felt so empty inside. She felt as if she'd just made the biggest mistake of her life, but told herself that trusting Joshua again would be the real mistake.

She didn't know how long she'd been sitting on the porch when a white van pulled up and the side

door opened to allow Sarge to roll his wheelchair out.

The driver, Jeffrey Canfield, walked with Sarge
to the porch stairs where he helped Sarge out of
the chair. He placed the chair on top of the porch,
then assisted Sarge back into the chair.

"How you doing, Claire?"

"Okay, Jeffrey, what about you?"

"Not bad." The young man flashed her a
friendly smile. "Sarge keeps me on my toes."

"Somebody needs to," Sarge replied.

Jeffrey laughed. "I'll see you tomorrow. Same
time, same place."

"You want me to take you inside?" Claire
asked when Jeffrey had left.

"No, I'd like to sit out in the fresh air for a little
while."

Claire noticed he looked more tired than she'd
seen him in a while. "Hard day?" she asked.

"I'm just worn out. Where's Joshua?"

"He went for a walk."

"You two fighting?"

Claire hesitated a moment before replying. "We
talked and things got a little heated. I imagine he'll
only be in town for a couple more days."

"So, it's like that," Sarge said. "I thought
maybe the two of you might find your way back
to each other."

Tears burned at Claire's eyes and she swiped at
them. She hadn't cried in years and today she

couldn't seem to stop crying. "I'm afraid, Sarge. I'm afraid that if I let him in my life once more I'll get hurt again."

Sarge released a sigh. "Ah, Cookie, fear is a terrible thing."

She looked at him in surprise. "What could you know about fear? You're the most fearless man I've ever known."

"Ah, but there was a time when I was gripped by the worst fear possible," he replied.

"When?"

"When your father and mother died and I knew you were coming to live here with me." Sarge leaned his head back and closed his eyes for a minute. "I'd just lost my only child and my heart was filled with a grief I'd never known before. I wasn't at all sure I wanted to raise you...love you and then have something terrible happen to you."

Shock swept through her as she contemplated Sarge's confession. She'd been a little girl who'd lost her parents and she'd never before contemplated the fact that when her daddy had died she hadn't been the only one who'd suffered the enormous loss.

Sarge opened his eyes once again and gazed unseeing in her direction. "Then I thought about what would happen if I kept my heart closed off to you and refused to allow you in and nothing terrible ever happened to you. That would have been the real loss." He smiled. "When you get to be my age, the only regrets you have are for the chances you didn't take, not the chances you did. And that's enough advice from a cranky old man. Would you mind getting me a glass of iced tea, Cookie? My mouth is bone-dry.''

"Sure. I'll be right back.'' She went into the house to get the drink, her mind whirling with the implications of what Sarge had just shared with her. She poured the tea then started back out the front door.

"Here you are. Sarge!'' The glass slipped from her hand and shattered as it hit the ground. Slumped against the side of his wheelchair, Sarge appeared to be unconscious. "Sarge!'' she cried again and shook his shoulder. A thin rivulet of drool escaped the side of his mouth.

"Claire.''

She looked up frantically to see Joshua hurrying toward the house. "Something's wrong with Sarge. I'm going to call 911.'' She hurried into the house and made the phone call, her heart jackhammering a rhythm of fear.

Please, don't take Sarge, she prayed as she hurriedly gave the operator the information. She hung up the phone and hurried back outside where Joshua stood next to Sarge, his expression stark and haunted.

"He's not responding, Cookie,'' he said.

At that moment the sound of a siren split the air.

## Chapter Eleven

They sat in the waiting room, frozen by fear as they waited to hear about Sarge's condition. Claire had ridden in the ambulance with him and Joshua had followed in the car. The minute they had reached the hospital Sarge had been whisked away, leaving Claire and Joshua to wait...and wonder...and fear.

Joshua sat in a chair, staring at a picture on a distant wall; Claire paced, frantic worry making it impossible for her to sit still.

Insulin shock. The EMTs had indicated that Sarge had gone into insulin shock. Please God, don't take him yet, she prayed as she wore out the carpeting pacing back and forth in front of where Joshua sat.

Her head felt as if it was going to split open as snippets of conversations whirled around and around: her conversation with Melinda, her fight with Joshua and Sarge's sage words spun like a cyclone wind in her head and she fought to make sense of it all.

She gazed at Joshua, who had his head back and his eyes closed. Love swelled up inside her, but that didn't surprise her. She knew she loved Joshua, had loved him since she was a young teenager and would probably love him until the day she died.

She sat down in a chair across the room from him, still looking at him. Even with the frown of worry etched deep across his forehead, he took her breath away.

*Had* she frozen him out? When Sammy had died had her grief been so selfish that she'd forgotten that Joshua had lost a son also? Had he needed to hold her to affirm their love and she'd turned away from him?

It had never been her intent. She hadn't known any other way to grieve. She'd learned at an early age that Sarge was uncomfortable with any display of strong emotions, and so she'd coped on her own with the normal anguishes of growing up.

She closed her eyes and thought of Sarge's words to her. *You only regret the chances you didn't take, not the chances you did.*

Please don't take Sarge, she silently prayed

again. I'm not ready to say goodbye. She wasn't ready to say goodbye to Sarge and she wasn't ready to say goodbye to Joshua.

Once again she looked at Joshua, saw the pain, the worry on his features. He loved Sarge as much as she did, so she knew all the emotions he must be feeling at this moment.

What would happen if she went over to him, sat beside him, perhaps took his hand in hers? Would it be too little, too late?

What would have happened if she'd gone to him five years ago, sat beside him, perhaps taken his hand in hers? Would it have been enough to make him stay? Had he already made his decision to leave her once again?

She thought of the picture of Sarah and Daniel and the last time she'd seen it. Sarah and Daniel and two children—four faces filled with love and devotion. A family.

How desperately she wanted to believe in that picture. How desperately she wanted that family to be her own and she wanted it with Joshua. Sarge's words echoed in her ears, *You only regret the chances you didn't take, not the chances you did.*

With her heart pounding, she stood. Joshua's head was now bowed, as if he, too, was saying prayers for Sarge. Her legs trembled as she moved toward him, afraid that she'd waited too long, afraid that it was too late for second chances.

He didn't move as she eased down into the chair

next to him. He did nothing to indicate he was aware of her presence. Couldn't he hear the pounding of her heart? Didn't he sense that this moment would be the defining moment of their lives?

She gazed at his hands, each one splayed on his knees. Strong hands, with long fingers—her husband's hands. If she touched him, would he jerk away as she had done from him all those years ago?

Drawing a deep breath, she reached out and took his hand in hers. For a moment it remained inert and lifeless in her grasp and her heart cried out. Tears sprang to her eyes and she was about to pull back when his fingers curled around hers, squeezing gently in silent reply.

At that moment, Wilma flew into the waiting room. "Where is he? What's happening?"

Joshua released Claire's hand and stood. "We don't know. We're waiting for somebody to come out and tell us what's going on."

"I was in the bathtub when I heard the ambulance. I dressed as fast as I could and got down here," Wilma exclaimed.

It was obvious she'd dressed quickly. Her blouse was buttoned wrong and she wore one brown shoe and one black. Claire's heart expanded for this woman who obviously cared so deeply for Sarge. She might be aggressive and opinionated, but her heart was in the right place.

"Here, Wilma. Sit." Claire gestured to the chair

next to her. As Wilma sat, Claire took her trembling hand. "You know Sarge, he's a tough old bird. I'm sure he's going to be just fine."

"If he is fine, then I intend to give him a piece of my mind for worrying me so," she said.

They all jumped up expectantly as Dr. George Wilburn entered the waiting room. "Dr. Wilburn, how is he?" Claire asked.

"He's stable." A wave of relief swept through her at these words. "He confessed that he didn't eat much breakfast this morning, then went to physical therapy. The exercise on an empty stomach apparently caused his blood sugar to plummet. We'll keep him tonight and monitor him, but I think he's going to be just fine."

"Can we see him?" Joshua asked.

"Briefly," the doctor replied. "I don't want him tired out."

"You two go ahead," Wilma said. "I'll see him after you."

Together, Joshua and Claire followed Dr. Wilburn to Sarge's room. Sarge looked small and pale in the hospital bed. His eyes were closed and he appeared to be sleeping. Claire slipped into a chair next to his bed and Joshua stood just behind her.

"Don't look so worried, Cookie, I'm fine," Sarge said and opened his eyes.

"How do you know I look worried?" she said and leaned forward.

"Just a guess. And Joshua is here, too, isn't he?"

"I'm here, Sarge," Joshua said. "And Wilma is out in the waiting room."

"Ah, she didn't have to drive all the way down here."

"She was worried, Sarge. We all were," Claire said, love for her grandfather welling up in her heart.

"It's going to take something bigger than wonky blood sugar to get me," Sarge replied, then sighed. "They told me they're going to keep me for the night. I don't want you two hanging around here. There's nothing more depressing than a hospital. Go home. If I need anything, I imagine Wilma will be more than happy to help me."

He didn't want them hanging around, but it didn't sound like he intended to send Wilma away. Yes, romance was definitely in the air, Claire thought as she leaned down and kissed Sarge on the cheek.

"You rest," she said. "And we'll be back here first thing in the morning."

"We'll send Wilma on in," Joshua said. Almost before the words were out of his mouth, Wilma swept into the room.

Joshua and Claire walked back to the waiting room. "Thank God he's all right," Claire said as they stepped out of the hospital and into the warm summer air. Now that the worry about Sarge had abated, Claire wanted—needed to talk to Joshua.

"Joshua…" she began.

He stopped walking and turned to face her, his features displaying a determination she'd never seen before. "I'm not leaving, Claire. If you want me out of your life, then you get the divorce because I don't intend to. I walked away once and it was the biggest mistake of my life. I don't intend to walk away again."

Tears welled up in her eyes as she gazed at the man she loved with all her heart, the only man in the world who could make her believe in magic. "Oh, Joshua, I don't want you to leave." Tears splashed onto her cheeks. "I want you to forgive me."

"Forgive you? Forgive you for what?" he asked as he pulled her into his arms and against his chest.

"Forgive me for being an idiot, forgive me for not realizing that I did freeze you out after Sammy died…"

"Shh." He placed a finger against her lips. "We won't talk about forgiveness. I should never have left. I should have realized that time would heal, and I should have stuck around and been patient."

He led her over to a stone bench near the hospital emergency-room door. He sat and pulled her down next to him, her hands clasped tightly in his.

"I love you, Claire. I loved you from the moment I first saw you."

"I was always afraid that you didn't," she confessed.

He looked at her in surprise. "Why?"

She finally found the courage to tell him what she'd feared in her heart from the moment of their marriage. "I was always afraid that you married me just because I was pregnant, not because you loved me. Then when Sammy died and you left, I believed I'd been right, that you'd loved Sammy, but not me."

"Ah, Cookie." He squeezed her hands tightly. "I was thrilled when we found out you were pregnant because I knew Sarge would let us get married even though we were so young. I was thrilled because I loved you, wanted you and the baby was just a wonderful dividend. It was always you—you I loved."

His words, coupled with the shine of love in his eyes soothed forever the fear that she'd always secretly entertained.

"Joshua, if we try this again, you'll have to teach me to open up more. If I had known how to do that, then perhaps you wouldn't have left when you did."

"I told you I'm not going anywhere ever again. I'll do whatever it takes to see that we share the rest of our lives together. Sweetheart, we suffered the most painful loss a couple can ever face when we lost Sammy. And in the fog of our grief, somehow we lost each other—and that would have broken Sammy's heart."

She gazed at him, her eyes shining brightly. "They're smiling down on us now. Both he and Caleb are smiling down on us from heaven right now. Oh, Joshua, I love you so much." She'd meant to say more, but his lips captured hers in a fiery kiss of need, of want, of love.

Claire knew a happiness she'd never felt before. As their kiss ended, she stared deep into his eyes. "Let's go home, Joshua," she said softly.

Within minutes they were not only home, but in Claire's bedroom, once again kissing as they helped each other undress.

The hunger between them was overwhelming, the need to touch each other, hold each other, make love with each other.

When they were both naked, they fell back on her bed, clinging together. As his fingers caressed her, tears sprang to her eyes, tears of joy. Finally, finally she was where she belonged, in the arms of the man she loved.

Their fevered foreplay didn't last long. As he took possession of her, Claire felt a sweet sense of homecoming. This was her man, her husband, her magic and she knew in her heart that their love would see them through the tragedies and triumphs of life.

A half hour later, they remained in each other's arms, sated but reluctant to move from their embrace. Suddenly, Claire remembered the picture of Sarah and Daniel. She jumped up and off the bed.

"Hey, what are you doing?" Joshua protested as she grabbed her robe and threw it on. "Come back here, I'm not ready to stop holding you yet."

"I need to show you something," she replied and bent down on her hands and knees to seek the picture she'd thrown across the room earlier in the day.

"What?" He sat up.

She stopped her hunt for a moment and looked at him. "This afternoon, after we fought, I looked at the picture of Sarah and Daniel and it had changed again."

"Changed how?"

"There were children, Joshua. The picture showed Sarah and Daniel with two children, a young boy and a little girl." She smiled at him. "I think the picture is a vision of our future." She bent down again to find the photo, finally spying it beneath her dresser.

She picked it up and hurried back to the bed. As Joshua wrapped her in his arms once again, together they looked at the picture.

Claire gasped.

"What the...?" Joshua stared at the picture, then looked at Claire, his green eyes filled with wonder.

The photo no longer depicted Sarah and Daniel Walker. Rather it was of a couple they had never seen before, a couple that looked nothing like the two of them.

Joshua turned it over and looked at the back. "It says, Joseph and Irene Woodson, 1868." He looked at Claire once again. "The current, the electrical warmth is gone. I don't feel it anymore."

Claire took the picture from him and held it between her fingers. He was right. Nothing emanated from the picture. She set it down on the nightstand next to the bed and turned back to Joshua. "Were they real...Sarah and Daniel...or are we both crazy?"

He smiled. "They're as real as they needed to be for us." He pulled her into an embrace. "I believe it was magic, Cookie, that the picture of Sarah and Daniel was sent to us to accomplish one thing..."

She nodded, loving the warmth, the love that flowed from his beautiful green eyes. "To remind us of how much we love one another and that we belong together."

"If it hadn't been for that picture, we might not have found our way back to each other. But we did and now that their mission has been accomplished, they're gone."

Claire placed a hand on the side of his face, loving the feel of his jawline and the faint roughness of new whiskers. "That picture might have been magic,'' she said as she gazed into his eyes. ''But the real magic is you and me and our love.''

His eyes darkened and once again their mouths sought each other's in a kiss that was, indeed, filled with the sweet, wonderful magic of love.

*Epilogue*

"Almost there," Joshua said as he and Claire made their way through the woods behind the city buildings. In one hand he held the tin box they had dug up nearly two months before. In his other hand was a shovel. They had come back to the Dragon Tree to bury the box containing the photo of Joseph and Irene Woodson.

It had been almost six weeks since he and Claire had finally resolved the past and pledged to spend their future together. That morning they had appeared before the justice of the peace to renew the vows they had taken so long ago.

He reached the Dragon Tree first and turned to watch Claire approach. As always, his heart swelled at the sight of her. She'd put on a little weight over the past month and wore happiness on her features as if it were a new form of makeup.

She reached him and smiled that beautiful smile that always made him feel as if he'd been kicked in the stomach. "The last time I came here, I was certain I was about to find a treasure that would change my life."

"And instead you found me," he teased.

She laughed, then sobered. "Why didn't we think of the treasure being buried by the flagpole at the fire station?"

"It just never occurred to me," he replied. The week before, Margaret Bratton had found the ten-thousand-dollar treasure that had been buried by Clark Windsloe.

"I'm glad Margaret found it," Claire said. "She's been a widow for several years, living on a fixed income and she has a heart of gold. She'll put it to good use."

"I think Sarge is going to ask Wilma to marry him," Joshua said. "He asked me last night if I thought it was foolish for a man his age to get married."

"What did you tell him?"

He grinned at her. "I told him I highly recommend the state of marriage and that one is never too old to enjoy it."

He held the tin box out to her. "Shall we get started?"

She nodded and took the box, then watched while he dug a hole big enough to hold it. When he was finished, he set the shovel against the tree, then took the box from her.

"Just think, perhaps a year from now, ten years from now, a hundred years from now, somebody will dig up this box and the picture inside will transform their lives," he said. He placed the box into the hole, then grabbed his shovel and quickly covered it.

When he was finished, he turned back to Claire. "What are you smiling about?" he asked. She had the most wonderful smile on her face.

"I was just thinking about the day I came here to find the treasure that would change my life." She stepped closer to him and wrapped her arms around his neck. Her smoke-gray eyes radiated a love that both electrified and humbled him. "I did find my treasure."

"The picture of Sarah and Daniel did change your life," he said.

She smiled. "Oh, Joshua. That picture wasn't the real treasure. You were—you and your love are the real treasure in my life."

Joshua's heart had never felt so full as he gazed at the woman he'd loved, at the woman he would love through all of eternity. He claimed her waiting lips with his and silently thanked Sarah and Daniel for giving him back his life, for returning him to his wife.

*  *  *  *  *

*Watch for Carla Cassidy's next release,
LAST SEEN...,
available in July from
Silhouette Intimate Moments.*

Coming soon from

## SILHOUETTE *Romance* ®

# Teresa Southwick's

## Desert Brides

*In a sultry, exotic paradise,
three American women bring three handsome
sheiks to their knees to become...Desert Brides.*

### July 2003
## TO CATCH A SHEIK
### SR #1674

Happily-ever-after sounded too good to be true to this
Prince Charming...until his new assistant arrived....

### September 2003
## TO KISS A SHEIK
### SR #1686

There was more to his plain-Jane nanny than met the eye.
This single dad and prince was determined to find out what!

### November 2003
## TO WED A SHEIK
### SR #1696

A nurse knew better than to fall for the hospital benefactor
and crown prince...didn't she?

*Available at your favorite retail outlet.*

### *Silhouette* ®
*Where love comes alive* ™

**Don't miss the latest miniseries from award-winning author Marie Ferrarella:**

The MOM SQUAD

### Meet...

**Sherry Campbell**—ambitious newswoman who makes headlines when a handsome billionaire arrives to sweep her off her feet...and shepherd her new son into the world!
**A BILLIONAIRE AND A BABY, SE#1528,**
**available March 2003**

**Joanna Prescott**—Nine months after her visit to the sperm bank, her old love rescues her from a burning house—then delivers her baby....
**A BACHELOR AND A BABY, SD#1503,**
**available April 2003**

**Chris "C.J." Jones**—FBI agent, expectant mother and always on the case. When the baby comes, will her irresistible partner be by her side?
**THE BABY MISSION, IM#1220, available May 2003**

**Lori O'Neill**—A forbidden attraction blows down this pregnant Lamaze teacher's tough-woman facade and makes her consider the love of a lifetime!
**BEAUTY AND THE BABY, SR#1668,**
**available June 2003**

**The Mom Squad—these single mothers-to-be are ready for labor...and true love!**

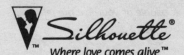

Silhouette®
*Where love comes alive*™

**From *USA TODAY* bestselling author**

# EMILIE RICHARDS

**comes the story of a woman who has played life by the book, and now the rules have changed.**

Faith Bronson, daughter of a prominent Virginia senator and wife of a charismatic lobbyist, finds her privileged life shattered when her marriage ends abruptly. Only just beginning to face the lie she has lived, she finds sanctuary with her two children in a run-down row house in exclusive Georgetown. This historic house harbors deep secrets of its own, secrets that force Faith to confront the deceit that has long defined her.

# PROSPECT STREET

"Richards adds to the territory staked out by such authors as Barbara Delinsky and Kristin Hannah…. Richards' writing is unpretentious and effective and her characters burst with vitality and authenticity."

—*Publishers Weekly*

*Available the first week of June 2003 wherever paperbacks are sold!*

**MIRA®**

# MONTANA MAVERICKS

## The Kingsleys

**A woman from the past. A death-defying accident. A moment
in time that changes one man's life forever.**

*Nothing is as it seems beneath the big skies of Montana....*

Return to Rumor, Montana, to meet the Kingsley family
in this exciting anthology featuring two brand-new stories!

*First Love* **by Crystal Green**
and
*Second Chance* **by Judy Duarte**

*On sale July 2003 only from Silhouette Books!*

Also available July 2003

Follow the Kingsleys' story in **MOON OVER MONTANA by Jackie Merritt**
Silhouette Special Edition #1550

*Where love comes alive*™

# COMING NEXT MONTH